MADRONA SUNSET
Madrona Island Series 1

BY JAMI DAVENPORT

Copyright © 2014 by Cedrona Enterprises

All rights reserved. No part of this book may be reproduced, scanned, or distributed in any printed or electronic form without prior written permission from Jami Davenport. Please do not participate in or encourage piracy of copyrighted materials in violation of the author's rights. Purchase only authorized editions.

Cover by
Hot DAMN DESIGNS
www.HotDamnDesigns.com

This book is a work of fiction. While reference might be made to actual historical events or existing locations, the names, characters, places and incidents are either the product of the author's imagination or are used fictitiously, and any resemblance to actual persons, living or dead, business establishments, events, or locales is entirely coincidental.

Warning
This book contains sexually explicit scenes and adult language and may be considered offensive to some readers. This book is for sale to adults ONLY, as defined by the laws of the country in which you made your purchase. Please store your files wisely, where they cannot be accessed by under-aged readers.

Email: jamidavenport@hotmail.com
Website: http://www.jamidavenport.com
Twitter: @jamidavenport
Facebook: http://www.facebook.com/jamidavenport
Fan Page: http://www.facebook.com/jamidavenportauthor
Sign up for Jami's Newsletter: http://eepurl.com/LpfaL

Welcome to Sunset Harbor, Washington, nestled on beautiful and remote Madrona Island where the main entertainment on Friday nights is a high school football game, everyone knows everyone's business, the pace is slow, and the residents wouldn't want to live anywhere else.

Meet a wounded warrior suffering from paralyzing guilt and woman pining for her dead husband--both damaged souls craving comfort for a moment or a lifetime.

DEDICATION

To Merilee for sharing her story with me and proving once again that truth is stranger than fiction.

A special thanks to Lori Wilde who helped me with the draft version of this book.

MADRONA SUNSET (MADRONA ISLAND SERIES 1)

Chapter 1—No Coincidences

"Three years is a long time to be dead."

Mandy Walters resisted the urge to scowl at her best friend, Carolyn Phillips. Instead, Mandy held her hand over her heart. "Funny, my heart's still beating. I'm still breathing oxygen. Worst of all, I'm eating way too much. I'd swear I'm alive."

Caro, her blunt and nosy best friend, glared at her. "You know very well what I mean. Just because Frank died, doesn't mean you had to die with him."

"I didn't." Mandy picked up a wine glass from the commercial dishwasher and hung it on the wine rack. She scanned the bar to check on the smattering of customers. No one looked her way.

Caro arched one black eyebrow. She'd been blessed with long, glossy black hair, thanks to her Nez Perce heritage. According to Caro, she came from a long line of Shamans; and while she knew nothing about the natural healing properties of herbs, she loved to talk the talk. "It's been three years. It's time to move on, to date again."

"What decent man in his right mind is going to date an overweight, dull, middle-aged woman?" Mandy stiffened and scrubbed the same spot on the bar counter, not looking at her friend.

"You're only thirty-one. That's not middle-aged in my book."

"Oh, so you're not even going to argue about the dull and overweight?"

"Well, of course, you're not dull and you're hardly overweight."

"I'm hardly thin."

"We've had this discussion before." Caro sighed, clearly exasperated, and a small part of Mandy couldn't blame her.

"And let's not have it again. My mother, my brothers, and everyone on this island has an opinion on my single status."

Mandy hated being lectured, and her friend's ramblings qualified as a lecture.

"You need to let go and date again," Caro insisted, in that annoyingly superior manner she had.

"I'm happy with my life as it is. I don't need a man to muddy the waters."

"You need one to warm your bed. Your life is boring. You didn't used to be like this."

"Are you serious? I've always been boring. I like boring. It's comfortable."

"No, it's a copout. An excuse for not living."

"I told you. I'm dull."

Caro snorted a very unladylike snort, stood, and walked to the door. Hand on the doorknob, she turned and, as usual, got the last word in. "It's time."

"Sure, whatever. I'll think about it," Mandy muttered under her breath. She almost smiled as she recalled the words of her Aunt Kat after her uncle died. *Honey, I'm just like your mama. I had myself a good man once. That's all I needed. Parker girls marry for life. We're one-man women.*

Her dad and her Uncle Harold died within a year of each other, shortly after Mandy had married Frank. Her mother and aunt never looked at another man. They immersed themselves in the church and their knitting club and God knows what else. They'd threatened more than once to start an internet PI service. Yeah, her mom the cyber stalker. Scary thought.

Frank should have been Mandy's forever love. Instead, he'd chosen a dangerous profession and paid with his life, leaving her alone to pick up the pieces and try to move on. Hopefully someday she'd meet a nice guy in a safe job and live the life she should've lived with Frank. Only she wasn't ready. Not yet. And some days she wondered if she ever would be ready.

Still, a girl could look. It didn't hurt to look, which explained why she'd glanced toward the door several times during the course of the evening. The Madrona Island

Veterans' Club in Sunset Harbor, Washington, where she'd worked as bartender for the last year and a half closed at one, fifteen minutes away, yet *he* hadn't come in tonight.

Mandy swallowed her disappointment, as guilt sat deep in her gut. There was nothing wrong with a harmless attraction to a handsome, mysterious man. Nothing. She'd never take it any further, even if she *was* looking, which she wasn't.

The tight-lipped stranger had limped into the bar for the first time two weeks ago. He came in almost every night, sat at the end of the bar, nursed one beer. He didn't talk much despite the efforts of the club's most gregarious members. She'd overheard enough to know he'd been injured in the Middle East and was going back as a civilian contractor in a few months, and she'd seen enough to feature his handsome face and incredible body in her late-night fantasies.

Mandy followed her last customer to the door and locked it. One-thirty AM. She thought he'd never leave, but she'd always had a soft spot for the vets and couldn't bring herself to kick out the lonely old man who'd recently lost his wife. She'd experienced the pain of losing a spouse firsthand. Even though it'd been three years to the day, the pain pierced her heart like it was yesterday.

She wiped the tables, put the glasses in the dishwasher, and counted the till.

"It's time to move on."

Mandy jumped and whirled around, tipping over her cash register tray. Coins splattered all over the floor. A dollar bill floated after them. "How did you get in here? The doors are locked."

The nondescript man smiled but didn't answer her. He was clean cut, of average height, with medium brown hair, and dark eyes reflecting kindness and sympathy, which happened to be the only reason she didn't hit him over the head with the nearest whiskey bottle in self-defense.

She couldn't for the life of her recall ever seeing him, even though he seemed as familiar as the aroma of her mother's pot roast on Sunday afternoons. But then his nondescript face looked like that of a hundred men, lined from too many hours in the sun, and softened by a friendly smile. "Sir, we're closed. You need to leave."

The man continued to smile at her with an otherworldly smile, which gave her shivers, even as her instincts insisted he wasn't a threat.

"Mandy—"

Her eyes opened wide at the sound of her name. She swore she'd never seen the man before tonight. "Who are you?"

He ignored her question and continued to smile calmly, sipping on ice water she didn't recall serving him. He pointed at her hand, specifically the wedding ring on her finger. "It's time to let go. Time to date again. Find someone to share your life." The man repeated his earlier words.

The hair stood up on the back of her neck. Caro had uttered those same words earlier. This was too crazy weird for her. "Please leave." She strode to the door, unlocked it, and held it open for him.

He walked to the door with an unhurried stride. "Let go. Frank would want it. You have too much love to give."

"You knew Frank?" Her hand froze on the doorknob. Her body shook and shock turned her cold inside.

The stranger stopped and nodded, still smiling.

"Who are you? I don't know you." She studied the man but couldn't place him as one of Frank's friends or acquaintances. She knew everyone Frank had known. After all, they'd grown up together in the same small town on the mainland an hour's ferry boat ride away from the island.

He nodded, his expression suddenly solemn. "You've never met me."

"I know all of Frank's friends." Mandy fought the panic that rose in her throat.

"Not all of them." His unruffled voice unnerved her.

"Leave, please."

The bar phone rang, and she crossed the room to answer

it. Wrong number. When she turned back around, he was gone. She tried the main door. It was locked. Unlocking it, she peered out the door, looked both ways down the street. No sign of the man. Locking the door behind her, she checked the bathroom, the closet, the store room. Nothing.

Mandy queued up the number of her brother who lived on the island but vetoed the idea. Calling Case, one of her overprotective brothers, would cause all three of them to descend upon her as soon as the other two could catch the next ferry, certain she couldn't handle her life on her own. Forget that she was older than two of them. It didn't seem to matter since she was, after all, a mere helpless woman, and they were men's men. Calling them would only add to their argument that she had no business living alone on this island, as if the place were teeming with criminals. *Yeah, right.*

Flustered, Mandy rushed through the remainder of her closing chores and slipped out the door, slamming it behind her. She looked left and right. The coast seemed clear. Sliding behind the wheel of her compact car, she started the engine and put the car in gear. Only then did she allow herself to breathe.

With shaking hands, she roared out of the empty parking lot, down the equally empty streets, and drove the mile to the Fiddler's Cove Inn, overlooking Chinook Channel—the currently inoperable bed and breakfast she'd inherited from her eccentric great Aunt Myrna's estate a year and a half ago. Situated on Madrona Island in Washington State's San Juans, the large older house had once offered premier accommodations for guests seeking refuge from the hustle and bustle of their lives. The property included Fiddler's Cove, named for the original owner who often entertained the townsfolk of nearby Sunset Harbor, the sole village on the laid-back island.

She parked the car in the empty gravel parking lot in front of the house. Sunny, her blind golden lab, greeted her with tail wagging and dogged her heels as she walked up the steps to the front porch.

Unlocking the door, she slipped inside with Sunny and turned the deadbolt.

She flipped on the light in the large entryway and left it on, then skirted around a stack of tile on the floor and trudged upstairs. It'd been a long, tiring day.

Hating herself for doing so, Mandy swallowed a sleeping pill, dressed for bed, and crawled between the cool sheets. Her cat, Marlin, took the opportunity to plop his fat ass onto the vacant pillow and curled up in a ball, purring his heart out, while Sunny slept on the dog bed on the plywood floor at the foot of the bed.

She tossed and turned. Her mind wouldn't shut off as it ran through the night's incidents, including her disturbing conversation with Caro and the even more disturbing conversation with the unknown customer, both of them echoing the same words all in one night.

Time to move on.

And those words reminded her of another disturbing stranger who'd been conspicuously absent tonight after occupying the same barstool every evening for two weeks. He was the first man she'd actually been attracted to since Frank, a harmless attraction meaning nothing, but proving a lot.

She was still alive. Still a woman with needs. And still lonely.

"Oh, Frank, why did you have to die?" she spoke to the shadows in the darkened room.

No one answered. Not that she expected an answer. She gathered Marlin to her and let his purring relax her until her eyes fluttered shut, her limbs grew heavy, and darkness finally claimed her.

A tone signaling a text message woke Mandy from a restless sleep sometime later. She fumbled for the phone in the darkness, scared awake, as she glanced at the large display on the bedside clock. No one called at three AM unless it was an emergency.

Unable to find her glasses, she squinted at the annoying device and held it a few inches from her face, trying to read the message.

Her blood froze in her veins as the words sank into her sleep-fogged brain.

Mandy Lou, I'm sorry. Let go. It's time. FL

She shot up in the bed, holding the phone far away from her with shaking hands and attempting to get a grip on the turmoil rioting inside her body.

Only Frank called her Mandy Lou.

FL? Her dead husband's name had been Frank, but her pet name for him had been Franco Loco. No one knew that. It'd been their little bedroom secret back in the days when beds weren't for sleeping.

With trembling fingers, Mandy pressed the Call Back button. The phone squawked at her, informing her the number was no longer in service, yet it had been no more than one minute ago. She tapped out a text message: *Who is this?*

A red circle indicated the text wasn't deliverable.

Holy crap.

She hugged Marlin to her chest as the tears fell. He struggled to free himself but eventually accepted his fate.

Yet this time his purring offered little comfort in a night full of too many odd incidents.

Chapter 2—In the Trenches

Brody Jensen was a coward, a fucking coward.

Sure, he'd fought in the trenches in Iraq, scrabbled his way across the brutal mountains in Afghanistan, and faced down insurgent troops with five times the firepower.

Yet this one woman scared the ever-living crap out of him.

Hell, it'd only taken him three years to track her down, and not because he couldn't physically find her but because he was afraid to find her.

Yeah, he was a coward.

Here he was—finally—and he'd done nothing more than grunt a few words to her each night.

Double coward.

For the past two weeks with the exception of last night, Brody had warmed a barstool at the Madrona Island Veterans' Club. He'd sit for hours, nurse one beer, sometimes two, and watch people. Especially one certain person.

He couldn't stay away, even though the coward in him wanted to run like hell and never look back, never face the demons who haunted his nights and his days. But he didn't, because something about her drew him back night after night and beat the hell out of going back to his rental condo and dwelling on regrets from a past he couldn't change.

She was the reason he was on this island in a remote corner of Northwest Washington State, but she didn't know it—even more proof he was a coward.

He stared out the huge picture windows at what had to be the most spectacular view he'd ever seen with the sun setting over the water, casting the adjacent islands in oranges and purples.

Mandy Walters bustled around the room, taking orders and delivering drinks with a quiet efficiency he admired. A good bartender was hard to find, and Mandy was one of the best. She might not be as fun-loving or cheerful as some, but he appreciated her straightforward lack-of-bullshit manner. Besides, he recognized a kindred spirit. Behind her fathomless brown eyes lurked the same pain and loss he harbored himself.

Being new in these parts and not prone to gossip, he didn't have a clue what made her or anyone else in this little harbor town tick. He'd come here to settle a debt to an old friend, even though it had taken him over three years to muster up the nerve.

Coward.

The curious stares of the other patrons didn't annoy him as much as they had two weeks ago. They'd stopped asking questions and ignored him after he snubbed their early attempts at conversation. He never talked about himself or his past. End of story. They'd figured that much out the first day, which left them to speculate among themselves.

Thirty-two years old, ugly burn scars on his thighs and lower legs, a mangled right leg, and walking with a cane, not the future he'd planned for himself. Yet, the worst scars were the ones that couldn't be seen—the ones which had eventually driven him here to make amends.

He didn't need the locals butting into his private business. Nor did he need any of the women who attempted to gain his attention. Not that he'd been celibate since he'd sustained his injuries, but his naked body repulsed some and earned the pity of others, and right now he couldn't deal with either response. He didn't need pity, nor did he need humiliation.

It'd been a year since he'd been with a woman, and he didn't plan on changing that any time soon. If his brooding and unfriendliness didn't deter the most determined of the bunch, Brody ignored them.

His focus stayed on one woman, and his intentions had nothing to do with sex and everything to do with absolution.

Mandy seemed like a nice woman, and nice women deserved safe, stable men, men who came home every night to their wife, two kids, and a dog. Men so unlike Brody and her deceased husband Frank. Men like Frank and Brody craved danger. They took chances. Sometimes they got lucky, sometimes they didn't. They lived life on the edge and once in a while they got too close. Frank had gotten too close.

Brody swallowed and cleared his throat, but he couldn't move the boulder-sized lump lodged in his throat.

And now Brody was left to pick up those pieces. He had his marching orders. His mission was get in, observe, develop a plan, execute the plan, and get out. That's what he did best. He wasn't a long-term solution man. He was Band-Aid man, who'd kept his promise even if it took him three God-damn years. In a few months, he'd satisfy his conscience and fulfill his vow to an old friend, then he'd be gone.

Mandy crossed to a nearby table, stacked the empty glasses on a tray, and wiped the scarred tabletop clean. Brody's eyes narrowed as a short peacock of a man rose from his table and approached her. Hair spray plastered the guy's hair in place. His fake smile screamed slimy, while the blade-sharp crease in his expensive slacks advertised an income way above the majority of the locals.

Mandy stiffened, her body language broadcasting her dislike for the man loud and clear. Brody's instincts kicked into overdrive. He sensed trouble. Leaning forward, he perched on the edge of his seat, ready to intervene if needed. The man pinned Mandy between two tables and blocked her exit with his stubby body. Brody frowned and strained to hear their conversation.

"So are you ready to accept my offer?"

"You know my answer, Kyle." Mandy stuck the tray stacked with empty drink glasses between them to provide a buffer and pushed it against his belly. He didn't budge. Not a small woman, she stood a few inches taller than the arrogant prick. Small-man syndrome wafted off him like steam on dog crap.

"Taxes on that much waterfront property have to be daunting for a single woman working at low-paying jobs, while a guy with resources could do great things there."

"Like tear down the old house, destroy the apple orchard, and build condos? I bet you know just the guy."

"A smart woman would be grateful for such a generous offer, instead of stupidly hanging on until the only thing she gains is a bad credit rating."

"This smart woman doesn't think generous is in this guy's vocabulary."

The man she called Kyle chuckled, obviously not the least bit insulted. "Figure it out. One way or another the property is mine." A slow, superior smile spread across his face with the menace of a snake slithering along the ground.

Mandy gripped the tray tighter. She stomped on his foot with her heel. He grunted in pain and grabbed her arm, jerking her toward him. The tray crashed to the floor.

Brody jumped into action. Well, hobbled actually, given his bad leg. In one swift move perfected from years of combat training, he slammed Kyle face down on the table, one arm cranked behind his back.

The asshole whined like the coward he was. "You're hurting me."

"Apologize to the lady."

"Hell, no. I didn't do nothing." Kyle's muffled voice betrayed his fear. Brody would be surprised if the bully didn't pee his pants.

"Apologize. Now." Brody gave Kyle's arm a jerk to drive his point home.

Kyle howled, and Brody bit back a snicker.

"Let him go." Mandy stood nearby, a combination of surprise and anger on her face. Surely, not anger at him, her rescuer, but then a woman's logic never made a lick of sense. Brody released Kyle, and the prick shot him a glare laced with equal amounts of fear and resentment. Without even a thank-you, Mandy bent down to pick up the broken glass.

Brody leaned over the whiny-assed prima donna. "Get out of here."

Kyle skittered backwards until he was a safe distance

away. Brody advanced on Kyle, and the guy almost ran for the door. Hand on the doorknob, his lip curled in a snarl.

"You're going to be sorry you did that. Both of you."

Brody rolled his eyes. "Leave." He added a measure of steel to his voice and pointed at the door.

Kyle didn't comment, but his frosty gray eyes burned an angry hole in Mandy's back. Whipping around and out the door, he slammed it so hard the old building shook to the rafters.

Several of the older men approached him and shook Brody's hand, stating it was about time someone got the best of Kyle.

Mandy said nothing to him. Not sure what'd just happened and how he'd manage to piss her off, he returned to his barstool and sipped his now-warm beer.

The mess cleaned and the place back in order, the remaining the patrons funneled out the door, still chuckling over Brody's heroics. Mandy moved about the room, collecting glasses, cleaning tables, and avoiding Brody. He drew in a deep breath and watched, unable to take his eyes off her.

Brody took another sip of his lukewarm beer and watched her. He admired her guts and could understand why his buddy had loved her. Sure, a lot of guys might not give her a second look. She wasn't stick thin, bubbly, or flirtatious. He found her comfortable, like the smell of his mother's cookies baking in the oven or the feel of a pigskin in his hands. He almost chuckled. He doubted she'd appreciate being compared to cookies or a football.

Brody rested his chin on his hands. Something about her drew him in. Not that he'd ever cross that line. She wasn't for him, despite the odd tug of attraction he felt on occasion. He definitely wasn't for her. Hell, he wasn't for anybody.

Brody straightened and signaled for another beer.

"One more, and we're closed," she said in her don't-fuck-with-me tone, and his mouth twitched in amusement. She pushed the beer across the counter to him. He reached for it and their fingers touched. A snap of electricity ran up his arm and straight to his cock.

He'd not felt such instant attraction since he'd been a horny kid in high school. He jerked his hand back in surprise. So did she. She stared up at him and their eyes locked. The grief, sadness, and confusion in her brown eyes sucked him in, crushed the very oxygen from his lungs while a flash of guilt squeezed at his heart.

No. No. No. He was a player, a danger junkie, a rover. She was a nice woman. Even worse, he owed his life to her dead husband.

His dick wanted what it couldn't have, simple as that. This would not happen. He'd find some other willing body to calm his boy down.

"Sorry," he mumbled and studied his beer.

She shrugged and turned away from him to straighten already straightened bottles behind the bar.

"So, uh, why are you working in a place like this?" *Lame question, Jensen.*

"Are you hitting on me?" Her hand shook as she poured herself a cup of coffee.

Aww, shit. Wrong thing to say. When it came to women, his expertise revolved around sweet-talking them into bed. He didn't have any idea how to carry on a normal conversation with a decent female. "No, I, no. Not at all."

She looked almost disappointed or resigned. Somehow, he'd said the wrong thing again. "I was just making small talk."

When she met his gaze this time, she'd pulled down the shutters and put up a "no trespassing" sign. "You've been coming in here for two weeks and never done more than grunted for another beer."

"So I'm feeling chatty tonight." He tried to smile, but recognized her grimace when he saw one in the mirror over the bar.

"Finish your beer. It's late, and I need to get home."

"Yes, ma'am." He saluted her. She wasn't amused.

Brody took a couple gulps of his beer and tried again. He needed to help her, not piss her off and drive her further into her shell. Yeah, he'd hoped to come here and find she'd moved on with some suitable guy and gotten her picket-fence dream. He could walk away guilt free, mission accomplished and debt repaid. According to the chatty waitress at the Dinghy Café, he wasn't so lucky. So now he had to figure out exactly how to fulfill his promise, and his instincts ordered louder than any drill sergeant that telling her the truth wouldn't get him anywhere but booted out of this bar and her life.

So he kept his mouth shut. For now. He needed more info on her and her life to find out where he could help the most with the least amount of suspicion.

She stopped loading the dishwasher and met his gaze. "What brings you here? Most tourists go to one of the other islands."

"I like the slower pace here. I need peace before I leave on another mission." He immediately regretted his use of the word mission.

"You're in the military?" She glanced downward as if looking at his bum leg. He knew what she was thinking.

"Civilian contractor. I'm a security detachment coordinator for World Security stationed in the Middle East."

"Oh." Her momentary thaw froze in a few seconds. He knew that look. She didn't want anything to do with a man in a dangerous job. Despite his relief, a twinge of regret poked at him.

"So you picked Madrona Island?" Her suspicious gaze sent him scrambling for words to convince her.

"Just seemed like a nice, quiet place to spend a few months. You know—fishing, hiking, that type of thing." He rubbed the back of his neck, trying to ease the tight muscles and almost squirmed. Hell, he never squirmed, not even under the most of dire of circumstances.

"I see."

He wondered if she was this suspicious of every visitor to the island. He held out his hand. "Brody. Brody Jensen." He waited for a spark of recognition, praying he wouldn't see it. He liked the feel of her soft hand in his.

"Brody?" Her brow furrowed, as if she'd forgotten something she should remember. She stared at their clasped hands and yanked her hand from his grasp, knocking a wine bottle on the floor. Luckily it was corked and didn't break. Mandy picked it up with shaking hands and pointed to the door.

"Please leave now." The anguish in her voice wrenched at his heart. He missed Frank, too.

"I'm sorry." The guilt sat heavy in his gut, weighing him down.

Her confused gaze narrowed on him.

"'Night." He pushed himself to his feet. His bum leg cramped up. He ignored the shooting pain, leaned on his cane, and hobbled out of the bar. She followed him. He heard the click of the lock as the door shut behind him.

This might be the toughest mission he'd ever volunteered for.

Chapter 3—Coffee, Tea, Or?

Mandy stared out the window of the coffee shop. Normally, a nice, strong coffee first thing in the morning brightened her day. Today nothing could make up for no sleep and two nights of tossing, turning, and haunting memories, not to mention the guilt and lots of it.

Frank always stood front and center in her dreams. But last night Brody Jensen's piercing pale blue eyes nudged Frank's warm, teasing brown eyes out of the way several times. An old man giving unwanted advice and a text message sent as a joke—even though it wasn't the least bit funny— planted these disturbing thoughts in her head. Definitely disturbing.

Brody stirred a fragment of physical desire she'd thought she'd buried with Frank. God, she missed Frank. His smile, his deceptive, easy-going manner behind which hid a driven man. They'd said the pain would dull with time. Instead, this huge hole grew like an out-of-control sink hole, growing bigger and bigger and swallowing anything in the vicinity, and that anything happened to be her heart. God, she really did need to move on.

"Wow, what's up your already tight ass this morning?" Caro tapped on her arm.

Mandy jumped, blinking several times. "Nothing. Just thinking."

Caro pushed a penny across the table. "For your thoughts."

"You don't want to go there." Mandy added a few more sugars to her coffee. So much for her diet.

"Oh, girlfriend, you know me. I always want to go there. Now spill your guts." Caro rarely took no for answer.

"You know the gorgeous stranger who's been coming into the club?"

"Oh, yeah, I know the guy. Walks with a limp, but he's still oh-so-fine. Nice ass, great shoulders, intense blue eyes.

Yeah, I've noticed. Just a little." Caro grinned and winked. "What about him?"

"His name is Brody, Brody Jensen. He got into it with Kyle, defended me when Kyle started threatening me."

"Oh, a hero. I love heroes."

"I can take care of myself. I have been for three years. I wish Brody wouldn't hang around there. He's too—too tempting." Mandy spit out the last sentence before she lost her nerve.

"Tempting? Then let him tempt away."

"I can't. Frank—"

"—never wanted you to be alone if something happened to him." Caro finished for her. "You need to move on."

A chill slithered up Mandy's spine as she recalled those very words. "I've been hearing that a lot lately."

Caro's eyes narrowed as she studied Mandy's stricken face. "Okay, you're holding back more dirt than your thing for the hunky stranger."

"I don't have a thing for him."

Caro tilted her head and raised both brows. "Sure you don't."

Prepared to do anything to distract Caro, Mandy told her about her two encounters. "After I spoke to you the other night about moving on, a guy showed up in the bar. I thought the doors were locked. But suddenly there he was like he'd materialized from thin air."

"And?"

"It should've been creepy but it wasn't. For some reason, he didn't scare me, but his message was disturbing. He said he knew Frank, told me to move on. Frank would want it. I turned my back, and he was gone. When I went to the door to check the street, the door was locked—from the inside. I checked the entire bar. He wasn't in there, and the doors were locked."

Caro blew out a hushed breath. "A Wyakin."

"A what?"

"A guardian angel of sorts. A spiritual helper."

Mandy chose to ignore Caro's statement. "There's more."

"More than that?"

Mandy searched for the text message and handed the phone over to Caro. Her friend read the message, and her face turned white. Caro did exactly as Mandy had done previously—she redialed the number.

Mouth open, Caro lifted her gaze. Mandy took little satisfaction in having finally rendered Caro speechless. Caro dialed the number again as if she couldn't believe the first response.

"It's out of service."

Mandy shrugged in an attempt to dismiss the eerie circumstances. "I did some research. I guess it's not hard to fake a number. It was a joke."

"A very cruel one by someone who knows you? I don't buy that. First the angel, then the text, and now you're attracted to a gorgeous hunk who seems interested in you. There are no coincidences. Everything in life happens for a reason."

"I need to find a way to earn more money," Mandy blurted out, changing the subject to another one just as troubling and on her mind as much as Brody was lately. "I can't pay the property taxes due this month. I'm borderline broke with no end in sight."

"Can your family help you out?"

"My family helps when they can."

"Which is never. Parker and Caleb live off island, and Case works two jobs. Besides, your family wants you to sell that place and move back to the mainland."

Mandy didn't dispute the truth of Caro's words. "I need to rent rooms, but the place is in shambles."

"What about the Bayview Room? Didn't your crook of a contractor finish that one before he bailed on you? And it has a separate entrance."

"How can I rent out a room to tourists with all the common areas in a state of construction?"

"Just rent the room. Put a sign up at the club and see if

you can get someone to rent it monthly; maybe one of our customers has family visiting or something."

Mandy brightened a little. "That's actually a good idea.'

"Don't sound so shocked," Caro pouted.

Mandy grinned at her friend, a little of the weight lifting off her shoulders. "How much do you think I can get for that room?"

"A lot. It's a big room with a great view of Fiddler's Cove, its own patio, and bathroom."

"It has a small fridge and a microwave, too." Mandy tore a piece of paper from her notebook and started scribbling down the text for her ad.

Renting the room wouldn't pay all the bills, but it'd help.

A few hours later Mandy pinned a colorful ad on the Veterans' Club bulletin board. If that didn't do the trick, she'd hang another one at the coffee shop.

* * * *

Brody rubbed his sweaty palms on his jeans. This was fucking ridiculous. Women never made him nervous, especially not a woman he'd already deemed hands-off. Damn, he could use a cigarette about now, but he'd quit smoking after Frank died. Frank hated smoking, and Brody had smoked like a chimney up until that fateful day. Ever since he'd been nicotine-free.

Steeling his usual steely resolve, he pushed on the door to the Veterans' Club and limped inside. Squinting into the darkness, he waited a few seconds for his eyes to adjust to the dim lighting. He hobbled to the bar, having forgotten his cane in the motel room. Choosing a barstool where he wouldn't have his back to the door, he hoisted himself onto the padded seat. His gaze swept around the room. A couple old guys sat in a corner watching the Mariners on the flat screen hanging on the wall. Another group played a quiet game of cards in the back corner.

A beautiful Native American woman filled a tray with beers and nodded at him. "Be right with ya."

A guy at the end of the bar sized him up like a man sizes up his competition. Brody recalled seeing him in here a few times talking to Mandy. The guy wore sweats and a T-shirt with a Sunset Harbor Wildcats Football logo emblazoned across his chest in orange and gold. Most likely a high school football coach. Brody knew the type.

Maybe he'd heard wrong. Maybe she had moved on, which meant she wouldn't need Brody's help. He could be on his way, guilt resolved because he'd done what he could. The prospect of leaving this little town appealed to him on some deeper level. Brody lived by his instincts, and his instincts warned that Mandy Walters might be more woman than he wanted to handle.

The bartender returned, practically floating across the room. He bet she'd be a damn good hunter with her light, graceful step. "What'll it be?"

"Bud Light." Brody glanced around again and lowered his voice, not caring for the other guy to hear. "Where's Mandy tonight?"

"She took the night off." The exotic female poured the beer from the tap. Foam poured out of the glass and down the sides. She didn't seem to care. She handed it over, even as the foam dissipated and left Brody with only half a beer.

Brody swallowed his disappointment, surprised that it mattered to him. But of course it did; he needed to repay his debt and get out. Already this small town smothered him. A new face around here was a novelty. Brody didn't like attention, and his presence attracted too much attention.

"Do you know when she'll be back to work?"

The woman shrugged one shoulder and floated off to wait on a new table of customers.

"Why are you asking about Mandy?" The man at the end of the bar eyed him with suspicion.

"None of your business." Brody ignored the nosy asshole.

"Her business is my business." The man rose and walked to stand behind Brody.

Brody turned and fixed the jerk with his best you're-boring-me expression. "Really? How's that?"

"She's my sister. That's how." The guy took a step closer, getting into Brody's space. Nobody got into his space. He tamped down the urge to show this guy exactly how much it annoyed him. Pissing off Mandy's brother any more than he already was might not be the best plan. He looked away, turning back to his beer. Being the one to back down was foreign to him, but he didn't need the complications.

He cradled his beer in his hands and stared into the bar mirror, expecting the guy to go back to his seat. Instead, the asshole settled into the seat next to him. "Perhaps your hearing got damaged with your leg. You're new to town."

"Yes, sir."

The bartender hustled back to the bar, no gliding this time. She reached for the surly brother's hand and patted it. "Calm down, Case. He's a customer, just like you are." She smiled at Brody. "Brady, is it?"

"Brody. Brody Jensen. And you are?" He held his hand out to the brother.

The man stared at his hand, as if contemplating his next move. He met Brody's gaze with an unwelcoming frown. "Case Knowles." He gripped Brody's hand so hard, he would've put a lesser guy on his knees. Brody was no lesser guy, even with his disabilities. He squeezed right back. For a moment the two men locked eyes, their hands in mortal combat playing their alpha game to see who'd back off first.

Brody didn't need to prove shit to these people. He loosened his grip, and Case followed suit.

"You've been hanging around the island for a few weeks, asking questions about my sister. What the hell business do you have with Mandy?"

"None. Just making conversation. I apologize if it looked like more than that." Just what he needed. An over-protective brother thrown into this already volatile mix. Hell, he'd come here to repay a debt, help out a lady in distress, or at least determine if she was in distress. He'd never counted on this town being so small everyone knew when the neighbor flushed his toilet or fed the dog.

The dark-haired woman slid a beer across to Case. Brody noted she'd poured the perfect amount of head, which irritated him. She focused her almost black eyes on Brody. "I'm Caro Phillips. Mandy's closest friend and keeper of her secrets." She winked at Brody.

He recognized an ally when he saw one. Brody winked back.

"Don't mind Case. He watches out for his sister. All her brothers do, but he's the only one living on the island."

All her brothers? Well, crap. How the many brothers did Frank's wife have? Brody searched his brain, but all the names and connections to those names swam in his brain in a big muddled mess. Frank's gregarious nature netted him a lot of friends. Brody never could keep them all straight. Most of the time, he didn't try. He just let Frank rattle on while he cleaned his gun or examined a map. "How many brothers are we talking?"

Case looked up from his cell phone. "Three, counting me."

Fucking wonderful. What he'd do right now to give his conscience the boot and get the hell out of this place, but the sadistic bastard hooted with amusement and settled in to watch him squirm.

"The Knowles boys take care of their own." Caro wiped up the beer on the counter in front of him and gave him another half-filled with foam. His pointed look at the beer then garnered him a clueless smile. He'd only been around Caro a few minutes, and even he knew she was anything but clueless. She was toying with him just for her own wicked entertainment.

Thank God, Case walked out shortly after without even a

backward glance at Brody. Just what he needed to complicate things, as if his confused feelings for Mandy didn't complicate things enough.

He drank the beer, paid his bill, and headed for the door, pausing at the bulletin board when a brightly colored flyer with the words Fiddler's Cove caught his attention. He scanned the flyer, glanced over his shoulder to see if anyone was watching, and snatched it from the bulletin board.

A second later the door closed behind him as he stepped onto the sidewalk. He'd just been given a gift, and he intended to take full advantage of it.

* * * *

Brody groaned and rolled onto his side. His damn leg cramped up again and pain stabbed his backside as if shards of glass were embedded in his mattress. Using his arms, he levered himself into a sitting position. His body ached from more than his injuries. The damn lumpy bed in this motel sagged in the middle and squeaked like a herd of mice nested underneath.

Gritting his teeth, he closed his eyes for a long second and breathed in and out, slowly and deliberately. Eventually the pain subsided to a dull throb.

He hung his head and stared at his scarred legs. The third-degree burns he'd sustained stared back at him in the form of angry discolored blotches. His left leg twitched like it always did first thing in the morning. How the hell those Army doctors managed to save it, he'd never know. Just before he'd passed out, he'd sat up enough to examine his leg. His lower leg appeared to be severed, except for a small bit of skin and muscle.

After several months in an Army hospital, Brody wandered aimlessly for a while. He tried to ease the pain with alcohol, but praying to a toilet every night didn't do it for him.

Brody shook his head, pulling his mind away from the

dark times. So a heavy dose of guilt later, here he was. And what a fine predicament he'd gotten himself into—his conscience insisting he pay his debt anonymously to his dead buddy's wife.

The slight tug of attraction to her took him by complete surprise. He liked his women small and petite and agreeable. She was none of the above. Granted, he'd been celibate for several months so perhaps to his dick, any woman would do. Not that Mandy wasn't a fine looking woman—she was—but not for him. Nor would he dishonor his buddy by having a fling with the man's widow.

Mandy needs a family man, not a guy who craves danger like you and me. Frank's words poked at him like an elbow to the ribs. Nor did she need a screwed up guy like him who could only offer her a roll in the sheets.

Brody pushed himself to his feet. He hobbled to the minuscule bathroom and splashed water on his face and brushed his teeth. Glancing up, he caught his haggard expression in the mirror over the sink. He'd lain awake most of the night trying to make sense of the conflicting thoughts ping-ponging through his brain, especially the ones having to do with Mandy.

And now he was going to attempt to rent a room in her house.

Stupid. Stupid. Stupid.

Brody fingered the piece of paper in his hand. He'd pulled it off the bulletin board at the Veterans' Club the moment Caro turned her back. Mandy needed a month-to-month renter. What could be more perfect than to help her out by paying his way and maybe doing a little work on the side? What single woman didn't need some heavy lifting once in a while, as sexist as that sounded?

Time to get his ass in gear. He looked up the address of Fiddler's Cove B&B. Since the island only had three main roads, it'd be a cinch to find.

Brody ran a comb through his short hair, dressed, and

packed his things, eager to get out of this motel with its crappy bed. He hauled his duffle out to his SUV and stowed it in the back along with his cane.

Presumptuous of him to think he could just show up and move in, but he suspected the woman needed the money based on bits and pieces of conversations he'd heard over the past few weeks.

He drove down a winding, two-lane country road—the only kind of road on this island. The lack of cell service rendered the GPS on his phone useless. No matter, he'd always preferred traditional forms of navigation. Just give him a compass and map any day.

About three or four miles out of town, he spotted *Fiddler's Cove Bed and Breakfast* on a sign and turned down a gravel road, which split through a grove of cedar and Madrona trees with the water to the west. The long driveway ended at a two-story white farmhouse sprawled on the shore of a private cove.

The view was fucking breathtaking, and he slowed the car to take it all in. The porch wrapping around the house framed a lawn badly in need of mowing. That'd be his first chore. Nothing improved the outside of a house quite like a well-trimmed lawn. He almost smiled. It'd feel damn good to be productive again.

He breathed a sigh of relief that her brothers weren't standing in the driveway holding a noose. Thank the great general in the sky for small favors. Case radiated some serious attitude, enough to give him a run for his money. He'd just as soon avoid any problems with him and her other brothers.

He parked next to an old compact car and got out. Grass and weeds grew next to the house and in the parking lot, fighting colorful flowers for space. Partially covered by a tarp, a pile of lumber was stacked nearby, along with a pallet of roofing material. Hands on hips, Brody frowned as he surveyed what appeared to be a construction zone.

The scent of horse manure drifted to him on a slight

breeze. He breathed out. Not being an animal person, especially when the animals were bigger than him, he didn't appreciate the smell of farm animals. A wire fence enclosed a good chunk of a nearby defunct apple orchard, and two horses grazed under the shade of the scraggly trees.

Brody walked across the overgrown yard to the temporary wooden front steps. A golden lab with a ball in its mouth trundled around the corner of the house, nose in the air as it sniffed. Dropping the ball, the dog walked right up to him and jammed its nose in his crotch. Brody backed up a step, but the old dog followed. Its grayed muzzle shoved against his privates. Damn, but he hoped the animal didn't bite. Reaching down, he shoved the dog's face away. The animal strained against his hand, obviously a confirmed crotch-sniffer.

Mandy opened the door and smiled a tense, not-happy-to-see-you smile. Well, hell, he wasn't exactly thrilled either, not with all the conflicting emotions she elicited in him, but he'd made a commitment, and he'd see it through.

Brody's breath caught as he stared at her. God, she had the most beautiful expressive eyes, even when they weren't exactly welcoming. He liked her curves, didn't mind that she was tall, at least five-foot-eight or nine, liked how her glossy hair fell down her back in soft waves. Hell, he even found the smudge of dirt on her cheek enticing. Obviously he'd interrupted her cleaning or gardening, judging by the state of her T-shirt and worn jeans.

Her scowl turned to amusement, and she laughed softly as the damn dog shoved its nose back in his crotch. Warm spring rain falling on flowers in a garden came to mind. What the hell kind of a comparison was that? He didn't think girly thoughts like that and prided himself on not having a romantic bone in his body, except maybe the one between his legs. If you could call being horny romantic.

Brody shook off this aberrant thought, chalking it up to lack of sleep. He grabbed the old dog by the collar and approached her, smiling his most charming smile. It'd been so long since he'd used it that it strained the corners of his mouth, feeling foreign and out of place.

"Brody?" Mandy's brows furrowed, as if she couldn't quite understand why he was here, even as she barely suppressed her wicked grin. "I see you've met Sunny."

"More intimately than I care to meet him."

Mandy laughed. He loved the sound, loved how it lit up her face.

"You should do that more often," he blurted out.

She frowned as if he'd stepped over some invisible line, which he had.

The dog made another lunge for his crotch, but Brody blocked his attempt. "Could you call him off?"

She raised one eyebrow and shrugged. "He's just saying hi. He's blind and deaf. The only thing that works is his nose. He'll give up and go away after a while. What brings you here?" She watched him warily as if she expected him to steal the good china. "Can I help you with something?"

He held the ad out to her. "I want to rent your room."

She stared at the paper. Her eyes lifted to his. He heard the catch in her breath, and his own caught. She recovered before he did and snatched the paper out of his hand. "I wondered where that went."

"Now you know." No sense denying it.

"You want to rent my room?"

"Yeah, for a few months. Not wild about the motel or the mattress."

"How do you know my mattress is any better?" The second the words escaped her mouth, her face turned bright red. "I mean. Uh, uh—"

"I know what you mean." He couldn't suppress his grin.

"It's expensive. A newly remodeled room with a killer view."

"I'm prepared to pay cash, two months in advance and a deposit."

"Two months," she whispered the words, as if weighing

her options. "Are you sure this is a good idea?" she said, as Caro sauntered onto the front porch carrying a cup of coffee in a Seattle Space Needle mug.

Caro smiled at him, one of those knowing smiles that tilted him off balance, as if she could read his mind and guess his intentions. "Brody. How good to see you."

"You, too." He'd best keep this woman on his side. She might be useful later.

"He wants to rent the room." Mandy glanced between the two of them, as if suspecting a conspiracy. Brody had no such agreement with Caro, at least not yet.

"Perfect. Let me show you. You'll love it." Caro took over as if it were her place, not giving Mandy a moment to protest. Caro led him up the rickety front steps, and Sunny followed with his nose pressed against Brody's ass. Brody held the screen door open for Mandy and Caro then closed it in the dog's face, ignoring his whining.

"I'll show him around," Mandy said tensely.

Brody stepped inside what was once a grand entryway and stared. Not only was the place in a state of construction, but Mandy wasn't exactly neat and tidy. The entire scene upset his compulsion for everything to be stowed in its place and nothing left undone. Sheetrock leaned against a framed wall, while other sheetrocked walls needed taping and texturing. In the living area, a couch and two chairs were arranged around a rug on top of an unfinished hardwood floor. Magazines littered the coffee table, and a fat cat lolled on a chair. It opened one green eye, then closed it, as if dismissing him as inconsequential.

A wall of French doors opened onto the back porch. Several yards beyond, water lapped at the low-bank waterfront of a private, sandy beach. A partially submerged dock ran from the water's edge several feet into the water. Literally.

Mounds of laundry were stacked on the dining room table. The kitchen nearly gave him a heart attack. Plywood on top of two sawhorses created a counter top. Rough plumbing pipes and electrical wires poked out of the walls at various intervals. A refrigerator and a free-standing stove crouched against one wall, almost buried by the surrounding chaos. A microwave on rolling cart occupied another wall, hidden among cartons of construction materials.

Mandy lived in this house. He couldn't fathom how anyone could wake up every day to such a mess, let alone live here.

"Are you in the middle of a remodel?" A remodel explained the state of the place.

"I was." She looked away from him, glancing nervously at Caro.

Brody's eyes narrowed, wondering what kind of contractor left a job site in this state. He looked to Caro, expecting the answers to come from her.

Caro pursed her lips and for once said nothing.

"How do you cook? There isn't even a sink here."

Mandy immediately went on the defensive. Her hands curled into fists, and her jaw tensed. "I don't cook. Much."

"Where's your contractor?" He knew he was asking too many questions, but he saw an opportunity here. He'd heard whispers around town about Mandy's financial woes and suspected she ran out of money during this remodel.

"I'm between contractors." Another quick look between the women indicated there was more to it than that.

"It's hard to get good skilled help on this island," Caro added.

Thank God Brody was handy with a hammer and saw. He'd stumbled upon his payback to Frank, but he had his work cut out for him. Damned if he knew where to start first, but he'd figure it out once he assessed the state of the entire house and made a list of chores to be done. His first chore would be convincing her to let him do the work without any payment. That'd be no easy task. She was a proud woman, and proud women didn't accept charity any more than proud men. God forbid if she found out who he really was and the role he'd unwittingly played in her husband's death.

"I'd like to see the room please."

"It's finished, not like the rest of the house, and it has a separate private entrance." Mandy's face colored from embarrassment as she led him around landmines of boxes and construction material.

Caro excused herself with a wave and disappeared out the front door, leaving him alone with his buddy's wife and his own lust for her.

She opened a heavy wooden door to an oasis in the middle of all this chaos. He walked into the room and did a three-sixty. Damn, he hadn't expected anything quite this nice after seeing the rest of the house. Another set of French doors opened onto a private covered porch overlooking the cove and the channel beyond, offering an incomparable view of the adjacent islands across the channel. The newly remodeled room was bathed in sunlight with a large four-poster bed and a small chair and ottoman, along with an antique dresser, everything in blues and greens. The adjoining bathroom was modern with a tiled walk-in-shower and a soaking tub. The stuff a guy could do in that tub with a willing woman turned him hard in an instant, especially picturing Mandy as that willing woman, her naked body partially concealed by bubbles and glistening from the water.

Brody raked a hand over his face and let out a groan.

"Is something wrong?" Mandy studied him with worry creasing her brow.

"Uh, no, nothing. This is perfect. I'll take it." God, did his voice crack or what?

"The price includes breakfast, but you'll have to eat other meals in town or cook your own. My private areas are upstairs, so feel free to make yourself at home downstairs, as best you can. I apologize for the construction zone."

"I'm fine. I don't need much, and this view makes up for any shortcomings in the house." He smiled at her, hoping to dispel her anxiety.

"Are you sure? I feel bad renting out a room when the rest of the house is in such bad shape."

"It's fine, really." He offered a friendly smile to reassure her. He'd smiled more since he met her than he had in the past three years.

"There's an old rowboat on the shore by the dock. You're welcome to use it."

"Thanks." He pulled out his wallet and counted out the correct amount of bills, handing the wad of cash to her, causing their fingers to brush together. The contact slammed through him with the speed of a high-voltage shock and just as powerful. Mandy jumped back, flustered, her face stricken with guilt.

Brody squared his shoulders and faked absolute calm. "Do you need a deposit? What about signing a lease?" He shoved his shaking hands in his pockets.

She gaped at him blankly for a long moment.

"Mandy?"

The sound of her name snapped her out of her trance. "This is…is fine. Thank you. Here's the key that unlocks your outside door. You can park anywhere you wish. The public areas of the house are, well, you saw them, but you're welcome to store items in the refrigerator and use the washer and dryer."

"Thanks."

"I need to run some errands. Make yourself at home." She managed a tight smile and nodded, hurrying out of the room and shutting the door behind her. A few minutes later she drove down the driveway.

Brody unpacked the few belongings in his worn duffle bag. Feeling a bit like a trespasser despite her insistence on the downstairs being open to him, he ventured into the downstairs living areas, clipboard in hand. He hobbled around the living room, making notes on his clipboard. He inventoried the building supplies stacked inside and outside the house and wrote down the tasks to be done, including additional purchases needed.

Once he had a handle on what it'd take to get this place into shape, he poured a glass of water and walked through the living room toward the expansive porch.

He paused at the massive stone fireplace on one end of the living room. Several framed photographs covered in dust cluttered the mantle. Frank smiled back in every one of them: Frank with a big trout, Frank on a horse. Frank and Mandy on their wedding day. Frank in uniform. Frank. Frank. Frank. As he moved closer, he noticed Frank's medals and a small football trophy from high school. An urn most likely containing Frank's ashes occupied the center spot on the mantle. The extent of Mandy's love for Frank shone in these items she'd placed on this mantle.

Brody shivered even though it wasn't cold in the room. Frank's hazel eyes stared back at him from his military portrait.

If it weren't for Brody, Frank would still be alive. If Frank hadn't left his cover to drag an injured Brody to safety, Mandy would still have a husband. A familiar surge of guilt rushed through Brody like a flooding river consuming its shores.

Reaching up, he gently laid the photo face down on the mantle, unable to face the accusations he imagined in Frank's usually laughing eyes.

Chapter 4—Upsetting the Apple Cart

Mandy turned off the car but didn't get out. Somewhere inside her house sat the most disturbingly attractive man she'd met in the past three years.

He upset the precarious life she'd carved for herself since Frank's death. Taking on a bed and breakfast in a state of disrepair and inherited from a great aunt hadn't healed her inside as much as she'd hoped. Neither would living in the past, a little voice squeaked from the depths of her disorganized psyche. She slapped down that voice and sent it scurrying for cover.

Over eighteen months ago, needing a fresh start away from the pitying glances of friends and family, Mandy, despite her family's protests, moved to this remote island where she'd spent her summers as a child. Case, having broken up with his long-time girlfriend, tagged along, accepting a teaching job at the island high school.

Frank's death benefits paid the back taxes with enough left over for an extensive remodel of the once-elegant B&B. Only a month into the project, the contractor disappeared, taking with him the last of her cash, and leaving her with an old, drafty house in various stages of repair.

Refusing to admit defeat, Mandy managed to get a job as a bartender while she planned her next move. Her family helped at first, but they were busy with their own lives. Besides, they disapproved of her plans and wanted her to sell the place and move back home. Even Case, who helped out when he could, pressured her to take the considerable money a sale would garner and run.

But she couldn't admit defeat, couldn't go back home where every bend in the road, every tree, every landmark reminded her of Frank.

And now she'd rented a room to a man who woke feelings better left dormant.

Worse than Brody's overbearing personality was her

body's reaction to Brody. Obviously, her rebellious body blatantly disregarded the notice she'd posted regarding the moratorium she'd placed on dangerous, sexy men in equally dangerous jobs.

With a sigh, she got out of the car. Sunny met her, nudging her with his nose. She patted him, pausing when she heard noise coming from the side of the house. As she rounded the corner, she stopped dead in her tracks to dodge an errant piece of two-by-four as it flew out of the garage.

"Oops. Sorry. I didn't see you there."

She opened her mouth to launch into a tirade. Her jaw froze and the words caught in her throat. Brody stood in the open garage doorway, naked from the waist up, sawdust peppered in his chest hairs.

Holy effing shit.

A thin sheen of sweat covered his ripped body from his broad shoulders and well-defined pecs to his six-pack abs. And that was only what was above the waist. His worn Levi's hung low on his hips and a trail of black hair disappeared in the direction of his fly and an impressive bulge growing more impressive by the second. Had she, Mandy, done that to him?

She jerked her head upward, not daring to go any further.

She'd never seen such a fine specimen as Brody Jensen, which was saying a lot since Frank, too, had had a fine body. Frank's muscles hadn't been as well-defined. He'd been smaller, more wiry. Brody's tall, lean body radiated sexual energy, a powerful man used to being in control, and something about the idea of him controlling her did a lot to her body, especially south of the equator.

She met Brody's gaze. A sheepish, apologetic smile flashed across his face, followed by a guilty grimace. Obviously, he too felt the sparks that arced between them. Like an errant ember in a dry field of grass, she stomped on it before it started a wildfire neither could control.

He grabbed his T-shirt and wiped his face with it. Mandy forgot what she'd been planning to say. He met her gaze, his expression closed and guarded. Seeing his walls firmly in place, she erected walls of her own.

"What are you doing?" She applauded herself on how steady her voice sounded.

"Can't stand being bored. Thought I'd do a little carpentry work." He avoided her gaze, cluing her in to something he wasn't telling her.

Mandy's stubborn pride kicked into overdrive. "You're a paying guest."

He scrubbed his hands over his face and heaved a very heavy sigh. "Sorry." His mumbled response barely reached her ears. He met her gaze. "I enjoy this kind of work."

"I understand, but I can't have you paying for a room and doing work for me. I'm not a charity case." She cringed at the pity lurking in his blue eyes. Obviously, he thought she was, and she didn't want anyone's sympathy, least of all his. Sure, she seemed pathetic to some people, living in a torn-apart house and unable to afford completing it and resisting selling it. They didn't understand. She'd had some of her best childhood memories here, memories free of the pain of Frank because he hadn't been part of those memories. In fact, he didn't like the isolation of the island and had only made one visit there the entire time they were married.

Mandy caught Brody's oddly wistful gaze as he glanced around the yard. She saw what Brody must see—a beautiful old place with great potential and a wonderful view, in a state of disrepair, a yard badly in need of TLC, and more than any one person could handle.

She stroked the diamond on her engagement ring, yet it didn't offer comfort as it once had.

Glancing up, she caught Brody's quick scan of her hand. Pain and remorse flickered in his gaze before he hid behind an emotionless mask.

He hurt, too, from some secret pain, maybe not as soul-deep as she did, but, perhaps in his own way, just as much. The thought struck her like a lightning bolt in a summer storm.

They were kindred spirits both trying to find peace in their current realities and survive tragedies of their pasts. A shred of compassion for this proud, damaged soldier wound its way around her heart. She wondered what his story was but didn't dare ask.

Sunny ambled over, nose in the air and made a beeline for Brody, who bent down to stroke the dog's fur. "He gets around pretty well for being blind."

"I suspect he sees shadows, but not much else."

Brody nodded, turning back to the table saw. "I'd like to finish this little job I started before it gets too late." Mandy almost gasped at the ugly scars running in jagged lines down his back, appearing to be caused by a combination of burns and deep lacerations. She swallowed and regained her composure, opening her mouth to ask about them, then snapped it shut again. The less she knew about him, the easier he'd be to resist, and she needed all the help she could get in the resistance department.

"I really can't have you working when you've already paid handsomely to live in a construction zone," she shouted over the sound of the table saw.

He turned off the saw and faced her. "Are you a good cook?" He smiled, his eyes crinkling around the corners and his white teeth a sharp contrast to his dark tan.

"Quite good," she admitted.

"I'll trade a home-cooked meal for some carpentry work any day." His engaging grin melted the last of her protests.

"I have to work at five. Do you mind eating early?"

"Not at all."

"You have a deal. A chicken casserole?"

"Love chicken." He winked at her.

Mandy retreated into the house as quickly as possible before her knees buckled, and she dissolved into a pile of embarrassed pile of female hormones at his feet.

* * * *

Brody spent the next few hours replacing rotted boards on the porch like a crazed hummingbird on steroids. Meanwhile, he glimpsed Mandy's rounded butt several times as she picked up the house, taking her time to inspect each piece of crap as if it were priceless. Not given to sentimentality, Brody would've chucked everything straight into the garbage. He champed at the bit to tell her as much but decided discretion was the better part of valor and kept his mouth clamped shut. These items meant something to her, and what she did with them wasn't any of his business.

He caught himself craning his neck for a better look as she bent over to fill another box. Her shapely butt was pointed right at his face. He swallowed and cleared his dry throat. Mentally smacking himself, he turned away from the window. What a poor, sick bastard he was to be ogling Frank's widow's ass.

Brody wiped his hands on a towel. Hands on hips, he stood on the porch and surveyed his handiwork. Not bad. Not bad at all. He smiled in satisfaction. The scent of something incredibly delectable wafted through the open French doors. Brody licked his lips, and his stomach rumbled. He rubbed it, realizing how fucking hungry he was and that it'd been twenty-four hours since he'd eaten last.

Mandy stepped onto the porch and whistled. "Wow, it looks great. You're pretty handy."

His chest swelled with pride at the appreciation in her voice. He nodded and avoided looking at her. He'd done enough looking earlier. "I'll start work on the house tomorrow."

"I can't expect you to work for nothing, and I don't have the money to pay you." She chewed on her plump lower lip.

Brody made the mistake of glancing up. He'd never been a weak-willed man, especially with women, yet he couldn't look away. His eyes fixed on that plump lower lip. He wondered what it would feel like to run his tongue over its length, suck it into his mouth, and nibble on it. Even better, what it would feel like to have that mouth do the same thing to a certain part of his body, hell, multiple parts of his body, in fact, any fucking part of his body. Brody's pulse jumped at the picture created in his depraved mind, while his cock sat up and begged for a treat.

Down, boy.

Time stood still. Honest to fuck it did. He'd never fallen for all that romantic bullshit, but as he stared into her deep, soulful brown eyes, a minute could've passed or an hour. Time didn't matter. Hell, he wasn't even sure if time existed.

She was beautiful, like a wild deer, strong yet frightened, fighting to survive in a hostile world. He wanted to make her world a little more hospitable and bearable, heal their mutual pain, and hunt for that ultimate pleasure. But he couldn't have the pleasure.

A strong smell woke him from his trance. "Is something burning?"

For a moment, she stared at him as if she didn't speak whatever language he was talking. Her eyes widened as reality sank in. "Oh, crap."

She ran for the kitchen with Brody close behind. Mandy hastily donned oven mitts and wrenched open the oven and smoke wafted out. His gaze slipped downward and stalled. He caught a glimpse of cleavage, really nice cleavage, the kind a hungry man could bury his face in and feast on for quite a while. He could lose his mind in that cleavage.

Mandy chose that very moment to glance up and catch him gawking. She straightened, sitting the charcoaled casserole on the stove, and raised her hand, as if to slap him, breaking the spell created by her fantastic boobs. He braced himself for the sting of a hand on his cheek, willing to take his punishment like a man. Instead she crossed her arms over her chest as if to protect herself.

"Sorry." He seemed to be saying that word a lot lately.

"I'm sorry. I burnt our dinner." Her voice wavered and

she hugged herself tighter. He swore she was going to cry at any moment, and he'd slay the evilest of dragons to prevent her tears.

Before he could stop his mouth, it spoke his thoughts. "Let's go to dinner. I'll treat. Give me a few to shower and shave."

Obviously torn between yes and no, he watched the battle play out on her face.

Brody gave her a gentle shove away from the door. "I'll meet you by the staircase in—" he glanced at his watch. "—twenty minutes."

She opened her mouth to protest, but he shook his head and escaped to his room. He stripped off his clothes and stepped into the shower. Brody leaned his forehead against the cool tile wall and wondered why the hell he'd invited her to dinner. The pull of physical attraction disturbed him. This was wrong on so many levels. She was a lonely widow, and he was lonely for a woman's warm body. If he gave in, he'd break her heart, betray the man who'd saved his life, and destroy his faith in himself.

Brody liked to believe he was a stronger man than that—and a better man.

Or a delusional man.

Chapter 5—Marching Orders

Mandy zipped in and out of the shower, showering, drying her wash-and-wear hairstyle, and putting on minimal make-up in about twelve minutes. Unfortunately, that left her with eight minutes to fret, a skill she'd perfected as soon as she'd discovered the male of the species in junior high. Once she'd met Frank, she'd honed it to an art, even after they married. She'd just fretted about different things, such as Frank's next deployment, whether they would have enough money, whether a uniformed sergeant would knock on her door one day.

That memory chilled her to the bone and proved the validity of her fretting.

She walked through the living room, specifically avoiding the mantle and the urn with Frank's ashes. Guilt plagued her. Whenever life got tough these past three years, she'd held Frank's urn and talked aloud to him, begging for insight or comfort. He never answered.

Yet, someone had texted her a few nights ago. A cruel joke by a person smart enough to fake a phone number? Probably. How could anyone be so mean-spirited? Unable to explain it, she chalked the call up to one of life's mysteries she'd never solve, along with the question of why Frank had to be the one to die. Why not someone else? Remorse flooded through her at such selfish thoughts. They'd told her Frank died saving another soldier. How could she wish one man dead to save another? Especially a man he'd given his life to save. Shame on her. Frank would be disappointed.

Mandy walked back into the living room and checked herself out in the mirror. She didn't like what she saw but didn't hate it either. She'd chosen to wear her favorite dress, a pink and green sundress that flattered her curves without calling attention to her too heavy body.

The thickness about her waist bothered her as did the roundness of her face, but she couldn't fix that now. She'd turned to eating after Frank died. Comfort food became her friend, and chocolate, her obsession. She ate both with reckless abandon. Until lately. The past few days, a different kind of distraction seeped into her thoughts, one with intense pale blue eyes and a rock-hard body.

A woman would have to be dead to not find Brody attractive, and she'd always been a sucker for a dangerous man. That's all it was. The little tingle she felt when he walked into the room was her body's reaction to being dormant for so long. All natural. It meant nothing.

Nothing.

Turning, she caught sight of her favorite picture of Frank lying face down on the mantle. The cat must have knocked it over. Mandy crossed to the fireplace and righted the picture. She stared into Frank's eyes and traced his face with a finger. A lone tear escaped down her cheek. She wiped it away, careful not to smudge her makeup.

Placing a kiss on her forefinger, she touched his lips. "I love you, Frank. I miss you so much." Just when she'd turned down that road to recovery, something shoved her back to square one. This time that something happened to be her hot boarder.

"Don't worry. He's nothing to me. Not like you were."

Brody cleared his throat behind her. Squaring her shoulders, she forced her face into a neutral expression and turned, wondering how much he'd heard. For a brief second, their eyes met before Brody looked away, but Mandy caught his haunted expression, and puzzled over it. He stood absolutely still, his hands fisted at his sides. He swallowed, still not looking at her.

"We should get going," he said, his voice quiet and a little raspy.

"Yes, yes, we should." She followed him from the house and slid into the passenger seat of his newer-model Jeep. He glanced at her, his gaze still troubled.

"You look nice." He averted his gaze, concentrating on

the gravel driveway.

"Thanks." Mandy fastened her seatbelt. Through a fog of grief, a remote part of her registered how surprisingly luxurious Brody's Jeep was with its leather seats, sun roof, fancy electronics, and of course, immaculate interior and exterior. On a soldier's salary, a rig like this must have cost Brody an entire year's pay. Oh, yeah, that's right. The man worked as a soldier for hire. Deadly job. Big bucks. A danger junkie, that one. Like Frank. The type of guy who craved excitement, especially the life-threatening kind. Another excellent reason to keep him at arm's length. Not that she needed more reasons; she had plenty.

Despite all her arguments to the contrary, her head turned, and her eyes drank in his profile. Everything about him screamed man's man. His rugged good looks would be right at home in an action movie or on the cover of a sports magazine. A cleft in his chin finished off his strong jaw. His imperfect nose indicated he'd broken it once or twice, but didn't detract from his pure maleness one bit. *Was that a word?* No matter. It fit. High cheekbones led to his best feature—and the man had a lot of good features—his pale blue eyes.

She'd never seen eyes that color. Doubted she ever would again. They were almost the exact color of the cornflowers growing in her mother's garden.

Those very eyes caught her staring at him. Heat rushed to her face and another part of her body as their gazes clashed.

"Did I cut my face shaving or what?" He redirected his focus to the winding road ahead, but not before she caught the glimmer of amusement.

He knew. Of course, he knew. Women threw themselves at this man every day of his life. He probably charmed them from his cradle. "Uh, no. I noticed your nose has a bump in it. Did you break it?" She mentally congratulated herself for a good save.

"Yeah, in football an eon ago." His deep voice

reverberated throughout the Jeep. She nudged the air conditioner up a notch.

Ah, something safe they could discuss. She jumped on it with the fervor of Sunny when he smelled steak. "My brother, Case, coaches the Sunset Harbor High School team."

"They any good?" A muscle ticked in Brody's jaw, almost as if football was a sore subject for him.

"Might be. Almost all his starters from last year are back. They play their first game next Friday night at home." Excitement crept into her voice. She loved watching the kids play. For two hours every Friday night during football season last year, she'd put her grief on a shelf and enjoyed herself. She'd never been the cheerleader type in high school, but she'd been one of the loudest in the cheer section.

"So you played?" Mandy asked.

He chuckled. "I grew up in a suburb of Green Bay. It's like growing up in Texas. If you're athletic, you'd damn well better play." Bitterness laced his voice.

"You didn't like playing?" Her brothers had played every sport. She couldn't imagine a guy like Brody not embracing a competitive sport.

"I *loved* playing. Thought I'd make a career of it actually. So did my dad." Another tick in his jaw.

"What happened, if you don't mind me asking?"

"I couldn't get it through my thick skull that no matter how good I was, college was a different ball game. In high school, they pushed me through. In college, I figured I could play ball and party twenty-four-seven, and the grades would be taken care of by some unknown entity. I failed every course my first semester and they booted me out on my ass."

"So you enlisted."

He shrugged. "Didn't know what else to do. My failure really pissed off my dad. We've never had much of a relationship since. He used to brag to his buddies on the golf course that I'd be the next big-shot Green Bay quarterback. Instead to him I was a colossal failure." She'd hit a nerve judging by his tight jaw and even tighter grip on the steering wheel.

"That's tough. And your mom?" Mandy needed to know more about what made him the man he was, even though she'd be better off not knowing much.

"She's a mouse, does whatever Dad says." He gripped the steering wheel so hard, his knuckles started to turn white.

"Brothers? Sisters?" She pushed onward.

"Three sisters. All highly successful and well-educated." The tick in his jaw became a twitch. She clasped her hands in her lap, resisting the urge to touch his jaw with a finger and stroke away his tension.

Instead she cut him some slack and detoured to a safer subject. "What would you like to eat?"

"I'm game for anything. As long as it's not MREs, count me in." Brody's jaw relaxed. He flexed his fingers on the steering wheel as if they'd gone to sleep.

"On the north end of the island is a little hole-in-the-wall called The Pizza Parlor that's the best pizza you'll ever eat."

"Sounds good." He managed a smile, and it relaxed his tense features.

Mandy smiled back. She *would* control the situation between them and keep everything purely platonic.

Her fragile heart depended on it.

* * * *

Brody held the door of the pizza parlor open for Mandy and followed her inside. He caught a whiff of her shampoo, something like wild flowers, a scent so uniquely hers, both innocent and sensual—one hell of a powerful combination. Brody groaned inwardly. Of all the stupid-assed ideas he'd come up with lately, taking Mandy to dinner won the prize. Even worse, he'd opened up to her about his failed football career and his disapproving, critical father. He never told anyone about his short-lived college football career, but he'd told her.

The waiter seated them in a back booth. The hushed voices of several diners masked each table's conversations, not that he was prone to eavesdropping unless he needed to do so for his profession. The smell of grilled steaks and garlic teased his taste buds.

"I smell steak." Brody sniffed the air.

"They have the best steak around." She grinned at him like an over-zealous tour guide.

"I thought you said this was a pizza place."

"Pizza and steak—the best—"

"I know. I know. The best around." Brody opened the menu, feeling mellow and relaxed. Two traits he rarely demonstrated or embraced. Tonight, he shoved his guilt in one of those neat compartments in his head, and let himself enjoy the evening. He scanned the menu and found exactly what he was looking for—the biggest steak in the house.

He glanced up to find Mandy looking at him with those deep brown eyes. Tonight the sadness usually lurking there took a back seat to a sparkle he'd only seen when she was giving him shit. She smiled at him, a smile direct from the heart, a happy smile. His chest swelled with pleasure, as he credited his presence for putting a rare smile on her face. Frank would be pleased.

Yeah, as long as he kept his hands to himself, his mind out of the gutter, and his zipper firmly zipped shut.

"Are you enjoying yourself?" He had to ask.

"Oh, yes, this is the first time in a long time I've been to dinner with someone other than my family or Caro. I love them all to death, but it gets old after a while. They coddle me too much." Her smile made her eyes sparkle. She really was beautiful with her expressive brown eyes, cute little nose, and high cheekbones. He didn't mind her weight. Hell, in some ways he liked her sturdiness in comparison to the starved women he usually dated with their hollow cheeks and jutting hipbones.

"Yeah, long time for me, too. It's been all about work. What do they say? Variety is the spice of life?" Maybe that's why this woman so totally not his type fascinated him.

"I guess. But there's a lot to be said about being comfortable and safe." She watched him over the rim of her water glass.

"Maybe for some, but not for me. I'm not one to put down roots. I like to keep moving, be it a mission or a place to stow my gear or a—" He stopped in midsentence.

"Or a woman?" She immediately blushed, as if she regretted the question.

"Especially a woman." He responded honestly, wanting to be perfectly clear about the type of man she was dealing with.

"The single women in town will be devastated to hear that, and some of the married ones, too," she teased him.

He lifted a shoulder in a half shrug, as the waiter returned to their table. "Shall we order?"

Brody ordered a beer and steak, and she ordered wine and a salad.

"Salad? When they make the best pizza and steak around?" He teased another smile out of her, which gave him immense satisfaction.

"You got me there, but I'm dieting."

He rolled his eyes. "Women are always dieting."

"This woman needs to diet. I'm too fat and out of shape for a person my age. I used to be so active." She ducked her head as if embarrassed.

He knew women, and no smart man touched that one. Yeah, she weighed a few more pounds than most women preferred, but those extra pounds did nothing to discourage his libido. "What do you do for exercise?"

"I swim at the local resort's pool, but not as often as I should. I like to walk. There are some pretty trails through the woods near the house. Frank and I used to walk in our old neighborhood—" Her voice trailed off.

He rushed to fill in the awkward silence. "I either walk or workout first thing in the morning. We'll go together. The buddy system. Stick with me; I'll get you in shape."

"I don't walk very fast." Another smile wiped away the sadness that lurked in her eyes moments earlier.

He laughed. "Do you think I do with this leg?"

She shook her head. "I bet you're a drill sergeant."

"Join me and find out." Brody grinned, even as part of him protested this latest stupid move on his part. He disregarded the warning. If he could make Mandy smile and laugh again, if he could help her move on, he'd be doing Frank an even bigger service than finishing the remodel.

In the blink of an eye, Brody altered his initial plans. *Finish the remodel* now became *finish the remodel and help her move on.* Not with him, of course, but he'd start scouring the town for a suitable guy. He knew just the woman to help him—Mandy's best friend, Caro Phillips.

By the time he left town in a few months, Mandy Walters would be fit, happy, and on her way to a life with a stable guy, two kids, and a dog, not to mention the proud owner of a lovely waterfront bed and breakfast with a full slate of guest reservations.

His mission would be accomplished, his guilt stowed away forever, and his debt repaid. Somewhere in heaven, Frank smiled down on him. He felt it in his heart.

* * * *

Mandy woke to some idiot pounding on her front door, and she knew just the idiot.

She opened one eye then closed it. The pounding on her door increased. She opened the other eye and squinted at the nightstand. With one hand she fumbled for the alarm clock. She found it buried under a pile of books. She threw the books on the floor and pulled the alarm to her.

Six-thirty AM?

She was so not a morning person. She worked in a bar for heaven's sake. She didn't wake up before noon. Ever.

The pounding persisted followed by a deep, commanding voice. "Mandy! Get up! You can't hide from me. In ten seconds I'm coming in. Get it?"

Overbearing, obnoxious, annoying man.

Mandy groaned and pulled the covers over her head. Marlin, her black and white cat, meowed from his spot on the other pillow, not happy at having his sleep disturbed, while Sunny snored at the foot of the bed.

"Mandy, this is your last chance." His singsong voice held a hint of a threat. She burrowed deeper under the covers. Surely the man would never break into her room. If she ignored him, eventually he'd go away and leave her in peace.

The pounding stopped. She peeked out from underneath the covers. Silence except for the ticking of the recently unearthed alarm clock and Sunny's steady snoring.

Her bedroom door opened. Mandy gasped and skittered back against the headboard, the sheets pooled around her waist.

Brody flipped on the light and studied her face. "You don't want to go, do you? You sounded serious about this last night." His gaze strayed past her face to her chest, obviously zeroing in on her ample breasts clearly visible through the thin material of the T-shirt she slept in. His face colored, and he looked adorably flustered, as if torn between dragging her out of bed, joining her in it, or running for cover.

She should've covered herself up, been her usual modest self, yet she hesitated. She liked the way he looked at her with lust glazing over his blue eyes. It'd been so long since a man had looked at her like that; even Frank hadn't after their first few years of marriage.

He continued to stare at her cleavage, his mouth open as if he'd forgotten whatever words he'd meant to say. His obvious interest made her feel sexy and alive and alluring. God, and that felt wonderful.

"I do need some exercise." She ran a thumb over her bottom lip and watched him suck in a sharp breath. What the fuck was she doing tormenting him like this?

His gaze snapped back to her face and his mouth closed in a firm, grim line. "I'll be waiting outside the door. You have sixty seconds." He turned all alpha-male.

Sunny raised his head and sniffed the air. Catching the scent of his current infatuation, the old dog crawled off the bed and waddled toward Brody.

"Ah, crap." Brody eyed the dog warily. He closed the door all but a few inches. One eye glared at her through the slit in the door. "Sixty seconds starting now. I'll be waiting downstairs."

He shut the door and started counting. *Sixty. Fifty-nine. Fifty-eight.*

Mandy considering jacking him around some more, but playing with fire would only get her burned to a crisp. She leapt to her feet, wide awake, and ran into the bathroom. She dragged a brush through her bed-head hairdo and dug through the hamper. She yanked on a ratty pair of sweatpants, a sports bra, and an equally ratty gray sweatshirt. Glancing in the mirror, she curled her lip in disgust. She'd better avoid the beach or she'd be mistaken for a beached whale.

Twenty-one, twenty, nineteen.

Mandy staggered out the door and down the stairs just as Brody reached zero in his countdown.

"I need a cup of coffee." She cringed at the whiny tone in her voice.

"That can wait until we get back." Brody stood at the bottom of the steps. One large hand rested on the bottom railing, the other held his cane. Eyes as blue as a summer sky looked her up and down. He narrowed his gaze, most likely assessing her current state of fitness.

They were the beauty and the beast, and she wasn't the beauty. Brody wore a slate blue pair of sweat pants and a gray T-shirt with not a wrinkle anywhere. The T-shirt hugged his muscular chest, a few chest hairs visible at the neck of the shirt. She licked her lips, wishing she could see the rest of his chest again. His short, dark hair begged for her fingers to run through it. While she was at it, she wouldn't mind sliding her palm along the rough day-old stubble on his cheek.

Hey, no one would blame her for enjoying the scenery. Nothing wrong with that, right? Still, guilt, her old friend and nemesis, squeezed at her chest.

"Ready?" His intense gaze scalded her insides.

"Yeah." She followed him as he turned up the long gravel driveway to the country road.

"Where to? You know the area."

"Follow this dirt road and take a right up the hill. We'll walk on the path through the woods." She hurried to catch up and walked beside him. For a guy with a cane, he moved pretty fast.

The summer sun was rising in a cloudless sky, promising a scorcher later in the day. Mandy huffed like the out-of-shape, overweight woman she was as they hiked to the top of the hill. By the time they got there, she'd perspired a gallon or more. Brody, on the other hand, didn't even break a sweat. Nor did he comment on her lack of fitness.

The path flattened out as it wound through a meadow. They walked in companionable silence, each lost in thought and enjoying the scenery. Below them, Chinook Channel sparkled like a blue sapphire in the morning sun, while the surrounding islands stretched lazily into the horizon.

Mandy slid a glance to Brody. He walked with relative ease considering his handicap.

"Does it hurt much?"

"Not much. Luckily I have a high pain tolerance. It's worse when I'm inactive for a while. Then it cramps up like a son of a bitch." His wry smile lit up his blue eyes and warmed her insides.

"How did it happen?"

His mouth flattened into a grim line and the sparkle left

his eyes. He stared straight ahead and picked up his pace. She hurried to keep up with him.

"I'd rather not discuss it." He spoke matter-of-factly, like a robot with no emotion, but she caught the now-familiar tic in his jaw.

"I understand. There are lots of things in my life I'd rather not discuss, but at some point, you have to let them out or they fester inside and fill in all the light with dark places."

He glanced at her. "Spoken like someone who's been there." It wasn't a question but a statement.

"Definitely. I'm a good listener if you ever feel the need to talk."

"I'll keep that in mind."

"So what do you do with the security agency you work for?" She flipped to a subject that might help ease the tension suddenly between them.

"I'm proficient in many of the local dialects in the Middle East. That makes me invaluable, crippled or not."

"Is it dangerous?"

He shrugged, as if it didn't matter to him. "I suppose. I don't think about it. The pay makes it worth it."

"No amount of pay is worth your life." She stared down at the wildflowers dotting the grassy path.

"If you have something to live for." His stark honesty shot straight to her heart. She recognized a lonely, damaged soul when she met one, being one herself. At least, her loving family smothered her with affection and concern. Brody didn't appear to have anyone who cared. Sympathy for this proud man surged through her.

"Do you have a home somewhere?"

"Nope, I keep an apartment in Phoenix, mostly as a place to store my shit. I don't like to put down roots. I like to keep moving."

The total opposite of Mandy. Except for the move to this island, she'd never ventured out of her hometown to live elsewhere, never wanted to leave her friends and family. Even when Frank switched from reserves to active duty, she'd stayed in her hometown, while he travelled to various places.

She took another path which led down the hill through an orchard of gnarly apple trees to a sagging barn and the last remnants of an old homestead. They both grew quiet as the path narrowed through a stand of cedars, madronas, and firs. Sunlight filtered through the tree limbs as birds sang and frogs croaked in a nearby pond.

As they headed back toward home, Mandy broke the silence. "Thank you for fixing the deck."

"I can do more than that. I'll need to inventory the supplies you have on hand, see what's up."

"I can't—"

"I know, you can't pay me. I get that. How about a trade?"

"I don't know what I could offer that would be worth the kind of work that house requires." She could offer him free room and board, but she'd already deposited his rent and spent it on bills.

As if reading her mind, he responded, "How about a free room whenever I decide I need a break from my life and come visit the island?"

Mandy mulled that one for a long moment. She wouldn't have to pay him back, and he'd get a free vacation to the island whenever the notion struck him. Surely that was worth finishing the remodel for her. "That's a deal," she accepted his offer before she changed her mind. The big, old house boasted eight rooms, not counting her living quarters. She'd gladly offer one to him whenever he visited. Once she started renting rooms, she'd be able to afford the taxes and expenses.

"I'll make a list and head into town this morning to get the most crucial items." His tone turned all business.

"I don't have a lot of money." Mandy kicked at a rock with her foot.

"Wasn't there a life insurance payout?"

"Yes, I used it to pay my aunt's back taxes and pay the contractor for the remodel."

"Let me guess, he took your money and ran?"

"He sure as hell did after he tore the entire house apart and only finished that one room."

"Why did you hire him?" Brody frowned, as if not understanding why she didn't research the contractor more thoroughly.

"I was new to the island, and he came highly recommended by Sunset Harbor's most successful realtor. I figured if anyone would know, he would."

"Realtor? That asshole who was harassing you in the bar a few nights ago?"

"One and the same. Kyle Winters."

"I wouldn't trust him any further than I could throw him," Brody said through gritted teeth, seeming to take Kyle's rip-off of her personally.

"Unfortunately, I wasn't thinking straight at the time." Mandy sighed, as she remembered how getting out of bed was the biggest chore she'd accomplished back in those dark times. She'd been dealing with Frank's death, and her great aunt's death months after had hit her extra hard. Needing to get away, she'd gladly accepted her inheritance and fled to the relative peace and isolation of the island.

"Even though I own the property free and clear, on a bartender's salary, taxes on all this waterfront are killing me. My family wants me to sell and move back." She hated to admit the state of her finances, which hung on a precarious thread.

"And you don't want to?" He stared straight ahead.

"No, I want to make a success of this place."

He shot her a quick smile. "I think you can, but it's a lot for one person."

Mandy shrugged. "I need to make use of the materials on hand."

"I guess I could try." His skeptical tone didn't bode well. "First thing we need to do is tidy up a little. It's hard to work under those conditions."

"You know, it wouldn't hurt you to loosen up. You're too rigid." Mandy bristled. They'd been getting along so wonderfully until he insulted her housekeeping skills. Granted, they sucked, but she didn't need him pointing out the obvious.

"I'm not rigid, but I can't work on a house where I can't see the floor beneath all the crap." He turned defensive and scowled, not appreciating her criticism any more than she'd appreciated his. *If you can't take it, buddy, don't dish it out.*

"Fine, I'll clean it up." Mandy stalked ahead of him. She hated him yanking her out of her comfort zone. She liked the mess for some inexplicable reason. She'd ceased to care about much of anything after Frank died. Now that she'd established a bit of a truce with her grief, she couldn't bring herself to change anything. She'd begrudgingly admit the man did have a point though, as far as being able to finish the house with all the clutter everywhere.

"Thanks." She heard the smile in his voice and found herself smiling back.

They finished the rest of their walk with small talk about the area. Brody loved to hunt and fish, just like Frank, so she told him what she knew about the island's fishing holes.

As they walked the last hundred yards to the house, she dragged her feet. She didn't want their walk to end yet. She'd enjoyed his company despite his tendency to be blunt and bossy at times. They rounded a bend in the driveway, and Mandy's heart sank. Case's truck sat in the driveway. Her brother leaned against the rear bumper, arms crossed over his chest, impatiently tapping one foot, and his eyes blazing with irritation.

"Hey, Case. Hope you haven't been waiting long." Mandy opted for a cheerful, clueless tone.

"About an hour, but I can see you weren't in any hurry to get back." Her oldest brother, and Frank's childhood buddy, ground his teeth together.

After gaining some distance from the G-words haunting

her life—grief and guilt—the pain flooded back at twice the strength. Her walk with Brody drove home all she'd missed these past three years. Unfortunately one look at her seething brother destroyed all the warm feelings from the walk and replaced them with loneliness and loss.

Not only did she have to fight herself to move on, it appeared she'd have to fight her brother.

* * * *

Brody limped the last few steps to the gravel parking area in front of the house. He leaned heavily on his cane and gritted his teeth against the throbbing ache in his leg. He'd overdone it and hit his threshold. Worst of all, Case's shrewd gaze didn't seem to miss a thing. Brody steeled himself for another onslaught of dislike from an asshole brother who obviously needed to get a life. Rather than live Mandy's.

After sizing him up, Case pointedly gave Brody his back. His snub shouted to the treetops that Case didn't consider Brody a threat. At least not a physical one. Hell, even with a mangled leg, Brody figured he could beat the crap out of him and his brothers at the same time. He'd put his martial arts and combat training to good use and wipe that smirk off Case's face after he wiped up the gravel with his body.

Yeah, he'd show the arrogant jerk.

Nobody dismissed him like that and got away with it—for long. At least they didn't at one time. Until his injury, men respected his physical prowess, never took him lightly, and gave him plenty of space. Now they disregarded him the second they saw his limp, which he hated with a teeth-clenching passion. He fucking hated how vulnerable it made him feel.

Well, he'd show Mr. Big Brother a thing or two. *Just name the time and place, buddy.*

Only Case didn't look his way to see the challenge in his eyes. Instead, he glared at his sister. One look at Mandy's flushed cheeks and radiant smile, and Case jumped to the obvious conclusion, the same one Brody would've made in his shoes.

Case didn't like what he saw one fucking bit. His entire body coiled into an explosive spring. He whipped around to face Brody.

Brody tensed, expecting Case to deck him, or at least try. *Well, bring it on, asshole. I might be crippled, but I can still hold my own against a dickwad like you.*

Despite his aching leg, Brody stood tall. His cane dropped to the ground. He stepped forward and widened his stance. Placing equal weight on his bad leg, he hoped like hell it didn't give out on him. He'd carve out an intimidating figure writhing on the ground.

Case held his position, even leaned forward a bit. The guy had guts, but then he assumed Brody was a cripple. They faced each other like a couple prime bulls. Brody half expected Case to paw the ground any minute. Good thing Brody wasn't wearing red.

He bit back a grin at that thought.

"I'm gonna wipe that smile off your face, asshole." Case cocked his arm.

Mandy grabbed her brother's arm and hung on. "Case. Please. What is wrong with you?" The alarm in her voice distracted him. He lowered his arm, but kept one eye on his adversary.

"Did he hurt you?"

"He never touched me." She rolled her eyes and blew out an exasperated sigh.

"I'll fucking kick his ass if he—" His warning glare backed up his words. This guy wasn't joking.

"Knock off the bullshit, Case. Think of your team. Their first game is next Friday. If you get arrested because of some foolish male posturing that went too far—"

Case's jaw worked as he considered her words. "But it looked like—I mean you looked like—"

"Whatever it looked like, it wasn't. Get it?"

Brody frowned. Suddenly uncomfortable as if she'd thrown a blanket of guilt over him, too. They hadn't touched, hadn't done anything. Yet he felt ashamed.

Case turned back to Mandy. "Mom thought you were going over to the mainland today to visit."

Mandy cringed at the censure in her brother's voice. Brody felt a rush of sympathy toward her. Getting over Frank's death had to be hard enough without her family's interference. "We took a walk and discussed plans to finish the house."

"Yeah, sure." Case shot Brody a warning glare. Brody glared right back. Screw this guy. He didn't answer to him and neither did Mandy.

"So did you just come over to bitch or did you want something?" Mandy watched as Sunny walked by, nose in the air, and headed straight for Case. Obviously Case knew the deal, he jumped in his truck before the blind dog located his crotch.

Rolling down the window, Case leaned out. "Mom sent me to make sure you're at Sunday dinner." He jabbed a thumb at Brody. "She says he's to come, too."

Brody faked a smile. "That's mighty nice of you."

Case almost growled his response. "Be there around two."

Sunny bumped his nose into the truck door and turned. Crotch radar at full alert, he located Brody and headed straight for him, tail wagging.

Ah, crap. Brody sidestepped the dog. Behind him, he heard Case's chuckle. At least the asshole found something amusing, even if it was at Brody's expense.

Case started the truck and drove down the dusty driveway without another word.

"Thank your mother for the invitation, but I'll stay here." Brody didn't want any part of a Knowles clan gathering.

"You've never met my mother." Mandy almost smiled.

"Meaning?" He cocked his head at her as he distracted

Sunny with several pats to the head.

"Meaning you weren't invited, you were ordered. Get it, soldier?" She jabbed him in the chest and walked into the house.

Brody stared after her, suspecting Mama Knowles might be the most formidable of the bunch.

Chapter 6—Desperado

The next morning Brody and Mandy boarded the ferry for the mainland, disembarked, and drove a half-hour to the small town Mandy grew up in and where the majority of her family still resided.

As soon as the door opened, Mandy's mother, Marta Knowles, swept Brody into a whirlwind of pure chaos. Obviously Mandy inherited her haphazard housekeeping skills from her mother. Comfortably messy, nothing seemed to have a place. Books were stacked on every available surface. Pillows were arranged haphazardly on the couch. A few years' worth of magazines were piled on the coffee table. Two little mutts flanked him like furry bookends and yapped at him every time he moved a muscle.

Mrs. Knowles plunked him down on a chair in the kitchen's breakfast nook. Her sister-in-law, fondly known to everyone as Aunt Kat, zipped around the kitchen, flour flying, utensils rattling as she whipped up a batch of chocolate chip cookies. The portly woman spoke with a southern accent, but Mandy swore the closest she'd ever gotten to the Deep South was Walla Walla, Washington.

"Brody, where do you come from?" Aunt Kat spooned the cookie dough onto a cookie sheet.

Brody opened his mouth to answer.

"How do you like island life?" Mrs. Knowles jumped in.

"It's—"

"We'd love for Mandy to move back home. She shouldn't be isolated on an island away from family and friends," Mrs. Knowles said.

Brody suspected the isolation was exactly what she did want.

"Have you done any salmon fishing?" Aunt Kat shot at him. "It's been a long time since we've had fresh salmon."

"Remember when Case brought us all those salmon he'd caught and we—"

"Do I ever, we ate salmon for a month."

The two women launched into an account of all the ways to cook salmon, laughing and jabbering.

Brody's head spun. Finally, he sat back and took it all in with an equal mixture of shock and awe. Mandy shot him a look of apology, but he caught the sparkle in her eyes. She'd set him up.

He'd been an only child with a father who worked sixteen-hour days and a mother who spent her spare time with many of her various causes. He'd never experienced family life at this level.

He pushed one little dog off his lap for the eighth time, not that he was counting. A timer went off on the stove and ended his misery. The ladies shooed him out of the kitchen and sent him to the family room. He shot a glance Mandy's way. She raised an eyebrow, her eyes filled with pure devilment, but she stayed in the kitchen.

Despite the animosity of the brothers, he gratefully escaped to the relative quiet of a pre-season Seattle Steelheads game, the local NFL team affectionately referred to by fans as "The Fish." Brody collapsed in an easy chair. He ignored the unwelcoming glare Case and Caleb shot his way. Parker offered him a beer. He could've used one or a dozen during the grilling.

After brief introductions, he popped the top and held the bottle to his lips, savoring the cold brew as it slid down his throat.

Three pairs of Knowles brothers' eyes dissected him. Sitting next to him, Parker, the youngest, clutched his beer and looked away first, as if he had no clue what twist of fate had placed his ass next to the enemy. Caleb, the middle brother, leaned against a chair back a few feet away, hands on hips, chin jutting out, and eyes hard as forged steel. Case sank down into a recliner and glared at Brody with undisguised animosity. The two little dogs sat on their haunches observing it all like referees in a contentious football game, expecting a brawl to break out any minute.

"You like football?" Parker watched with the intensity of a scientist conducting a research study.

"Some."

"If you're gonna survive in this household, you'd better learn to love it."

"Thanks for the advice." Brody didn't consider himself a member of their household, or even a welcome guest.

Parker turned back to the game. Brody sat in ignored silence for the next hour or so, a stark contrast to the older women's constant jabbering. Smells of homemade pot roast snuck into the room, invaded his senses, and reminded him he'd forgotten to eat breakfast. His stomach growled in response. He grabbed another beer from the small bar fridge in the corner, pacing himself. No one paid any attention to him. Leaning against the desk in the corner, he looked around the messy room with its well-worn cozy furniture, the epitome of casual and so not his style. Not that he had a style that didn't revolve around camouflage and sand dunes.

Mandy peeked around the doorway to the kitchen and motioned to him. Grateful for the rescue, he rose to stand by her side, feeling the brothers' eyes on him.

"Are they treating you okay?" Mandy glanced sharply at her brothers as she lowered her voice for his ears only.

"They're pretending I don't exist."

"Oh, good." She blew out a breath.

"My thoughts exactly. Are they always like this?"

"Yes. Except with—" Her voice trailed off. Brody wondered who really married Frank—Mandy or her entire family. The little rat dogs pawed at his legs. He glared down at them.

"Not much of an animal person, are you?"

"Never had to be."

Her eyes filled with sympathy, as if it was a bad thing not to grow up with animals. He didn't think he'd missed anything. He nudged the dogs away gently with his foot.

Brody's stomach rumbled again. Mandy laughed. He liked the sound of her laugh, like Christmas bells and apple pie and all that small-town stuff.

Crossing the room, she absconded with a bowl of chips previously hoarded by her brothers and sat it on top of the desk. He dug in, starving. "Don't ruin your appetite."

"No chance of that."

"Good, Aunt Kat makes a mean pot roast."

"I'm counting on it." He couldn't remember the last time he'd eaten a home-cooked meal. Much to his surprise, he looked forward to it. They seated him at the big table between Mandy and Parker. At first he was relieved until he realized Caleb and Case sat across from him. The two older brothers cranked up the intensity on their glares. Fuck them. As famished as he was, no one could ruin his appetite.

Aunt Kat said grace, brief and to the point.

Brody heaped his plate with every dish passed his way then dug in with the gusto of a starving man. The food rivaled anything he'd ever eaten. He didn't come up for air until he'd cleaned his plate, mopping up the last bit of gravy with the homemade bread. He recalled Frank's accounts of the Knowles family's legendary Sunday dinners. Even though given to embellishment, Frank hit this topic on the nose. In fact, the food surpassed Brody's expectations.

Aunt Kat tore the platter of roast from Caleb's hands and passed it to Brody. "You're a little thin, young man. Eat up. No one leaves this table hungry."

"He could wait his turn," Caleb pouted.

Brody flipped off Caleb under the table. Not that the jerk could see his finger, but the gesture gave Brody a measure of childish satisfaction. Caleb shifted in his chair to grab the vegetable bowl.

"Mind your manners, mister." Aunt Kat swatted at Caleb, who lowered his head and muttered something unintelligible.

Brody's thigh rubbed against Mandy's at the crowded table. Mandy's face flushed red as she glanced at him from beneath her lashes. She moved her leg away. The fork halfway to Brody's mouth froze in midair. His throat constricted. To his horror, his hand shook. He lowered the fork full of food and rested it on his plate. A quick glance around the room to see if anyone noticed brought him eye-to-eye with Caleb.

Caleb's eyes glowed with pent-up dislike. He nodded toward his sister and mouthed the words, *hands off.* Brody rolled his eyes. He couldn't resist. Mandy's brothers were too over the top to be believed.

"Is something wrong, boys?" Mrs. Knowles didn't miss a thing.

"Nope, Mom. Nothing." Caleb smiled at Brody. "Just a secret between us."

"I'm so glad you boys are getting along so well."

Brody almost choked on his food. Who was she kidding? "Oh, yeah, best of buddies."

Caleb's lip curled, while Case coughed. Mandy kept her head down. Parker pretended as if none of them existed.

"Brody, a strapping young man like you must have played some football."

Mandy glanced up, a wicked gleam in her eye, and answered for him. "He did, Mom. Played a little college ball at Michigan."

"You did now, did you?" Mrs. Knowles grinned.

Brody proceeded cautiously. Something was up. "Yes, ma'am. One year."

"Washed out, huh?" Caleb jumped on his words.

"Big head. Bad grades." Brody chewed on a piece of roast and showed no emotion.

"What position did you play?" Aunt Kat piled his plate with another helping of pot roast and gravy.

"Quarterback."

"Oh, that's perfect. Isn't it, Case?"

Case's gaze darted from one woman to another then settled on Brody. "Yeah, sure, whatever."

"You need backfield help on the team. You said it

yourself a day ago, but there's no money to hire another coach." Mrs. Knowles winked at her son.

"Even if there was money, Case said he didn't know of a qualified person in the area. But now Brody shows up like a gift from heaven." Aunt Kat winked at her sister-in-law.

Brody choked on his food, grabbed his water and gulped it down. The entire table hushed, all eyes on him. Even Parker looked up with curiosity.

"I'm sure Brody has better things to do than help coach a small-town football team," Case said.

Brody opened his mouth to agree. That'd be a first—him agreeing with Case.

Mrs. Knowles dived right in. "Brody's here to vacation, and he's agreed to help Mandy finish the remodel. He can't work all day, and his hours are flexible. This'll be a welcome break."

"I really don't think—" Brody held up a hand, tried to get the women's attention.

"Oh, pish, you'll love it." Marta Knowles nodded with satisfaction.

"What a great idea, Marts. We'll win the league for sure." Aunt Kat held up her glass and the two women clinked glasses of wine.

"League? Shoot higher. Regionals."

"State Semis."

"State. We'll be state champions."

"I'll start knitting those championship scarves, navy and gold with the state of Washington on them."

"I'll plan the awards banquet."

Case's mouth dropped open and stayed there. The guy looked shell-shocked. Brody understood the feeling.

"Ladies, I—Really, thanks but—" Brody stuttered like a kid on his first date. These two older women didn't seem to give a shit what he thought.

"Mom, you're getting ahead of—"

"Nonsense. It's all planned out. Brody's the missing

piece."

Brody preferred to stay missing.

Mandy nudged him. He met her eyes, begging for help. She shook her head. "No use. You're screwed," she whispered then leaned back to enjoy his discomfort, as evil as the rest of the Knowles women.

Like a spectator in his own life, Brody watched from the stands as these two women plotted his next three months and Case's. They chattered non-stop as they cleared the table, served dessert—excellent apple pie by the way—and sent the family on their way, while they organized a phone tree to the booster club members to tell everyone about the new coach and make plans for a big season.

Brody staggered out of the house to his SUV, not really knowing what hit him. He'd been taken down by the pride of the knitting club, when the best soldiers in the world had failed.

Mandy settled in the passenger seat next to him. She fastened her seatbelt and stared straight ahead. He said nothing and pulled onto the country road.

A strangled cry caught his attention. He slowed and looked over at Mandy. She shoved her knuckles in her mouth. A couple tears ran down her face.

Oh, crap. Women. What the hell happened that got her so upset?

"Are you okay?"

Another strangled cry.

"Mandy?" He patted her hand then thought better of touching her.

She gurgled like a baby.

"What's wrong?"

Her entire body shook. Then she met his eyes.

Well, hell. She wasn't crying. She was laughing. At him. Hysterically for that matter. He didn't find his predicament funny one damn bit.

* * * *

Mandy couldn't hold back anymore. She grasped the dashboard, threw back her head, and laughed until her stomach hurt. She laughed so hard she almost peed her pants. Holding her stomach, she chanced a look at Brody and the laughter bubbled to the surface again.

His brows dipped into a stern frown and he screwed his lips to one side. He looked adorably thunderstruck, like he'd been parachuted into a foreign land where he didn't speak the language, understand the customs, or have a clue why the hell he'd been dropped there. Her aunt and mother had that effect on people.

She'd bet being helpless rarely happened to a man like him. Of course, he'd never met the elder Knowles women until now. Heck, after all these years, they still had that effect on her obnoxious brothers.

Brody cast an annoyed glance in her direction then stared straight ahead, driving his Jeep off the ferry and turning toward home. That tell-tale muscle jerked in his jaw.

Gasping for air, she attempted to staunch the laughter.

Brody didn't appear to like being laughed at any more than he appreciated being railroaded.

"I don't see what's so funny." He clenched his jaw and gripped the steering wheel.

"You would if you were sitting where I am." She hiccupped.

"Well, I'm not." He drove up her driveway a little too fast and braked at the front door. Dust swirled around the car and engulfed poor old Sunny who sat patiently near the front door, lying in wait.

Mandy raised her eyebrows. "A little testy, aren't we?"

"I'm not good with kids." He opened the car door and got out, limping toward the private entrance to his room.

Mandy jumped out and hurried after him. "You'll learn."

"No thanks. Not why I'm here." He stood on the porch

and stared at a point in the distance. His face hardened into an impenetrable mask, but she read him like a military manual.

"Tell that to Mom and Aunt Kat." *And good luck with that, buddy.*

"Case isn't on board." His switch in tactics didn't throw her off.

"Maybe. But he knows his weaknesses. He's a defensive guy. He sorely needs a backfield coach. That would be you." She bit the inside of her cheek to prevent a giggle. Damn, but she found his discomfort amusing. Even worse, enticing. His weaknesses sucked her in more than his strengths.

Brody opened the door and stared back at her. "You working tonight?"

"Nope, tomorrow."

"I'll drive you."

"No need. I can handle driving myself. I have for years."

He shrugged, appearing to be battling some inner demon. "What time?"

"Four PM. Won't I see you tomorrow for breakfast?" Her gaze zeroed in on his big hand gripping the doorknob.

"I have supplies to buy. Won't be back till later. We'll resume our walks on Tuesday."

"Forced marches."

"Whatever you want to call them. In the meantime, straighten up the house, would you, please?"

She snapped to attention and saluted him. "Yes, sir."

Brody rolled his eyes and closed the door.

For a moment she'd deluded herself into believing he might actually like her. Men like him fell for beautiful women with great figures. She didn't qualify, which should make him safe to a point. He'd certainly eyed her breasts earlier. They were two lonely people using each other as harmless distractions.

Yeah, that was all.

Her memories of Frank kept her warm at night. One wounded warrior in her life was enough, even if he happened to reside in heaven.

* * * *

Old habits died hard.

Brody sat at the far end of the bar where he could see the door and most of the patrons. A good solider never had his back to the door.

Mandy rushed around the room, handling the large crowd with efficient ease, considering it was bingo night. The blue-haired ladies huddled around their tables full of bingo cards. Their geriatric husbands gathered around the bar and swapped war stories. Every once in a while, one would glance his way and try to involve him in the convo. Brody grunted as politely as a guy could grunt and kept to himself.

Since they loved to speculate on what his story was, and he figured the fantasy far outweighed the reality, why ruin a good mystery?

One guy, Harvey, didn't discourage so easily. He seemed younger than most; Brody figured him to be a Vietnam era veteran. He boasted an eye patch, a thin, wiry body, and a penchant for show tunes on karaoke night.

On this particular night, Harvey slid onto the vacant barstool next to Brody and signaled Mandy for a beer. She slid it across to him and slanted Brody a warning glance. Harvey liked to talk. Brody didn't.

Brody sighed. The guy started in on a story about his time in the Navy. His stories didn't require any input on Brody's part so his attention wandered to Mandy as she joked with a few of the patrons. A smile tugged a corner of his mouth as he watched her work her magic on the older crowd. They loved her and her no-nonsense attitude, tempered with a true affection for the senior citizens. She sympathized with their financial woes and health issues and never tired of their stories. If only he could be half the person she was.

A little sliver of pride slipped through him, even if he

didn't have a right to such feelings.

Case sat down next to Harvey and grunted hello. He had the grunting thing down as well as Brody did. After a few minutes, Harvey finished his story and wandered outside for a smoke.

Case mumbled something Brody didn't catch. "Excuse me?"

"I said the background check came back fine. You're cleared to coach."

"You disappointed?"

Case didn't respond to his question. "We start practice at three." Case stared straight ahead. He might as well have been talking to the bottles lined up on the mirrored bar wall.

"Tomorrow?"

"Yeah. Be there."

"Why?"

"You met my mother and aunt." Case spoke with dry humor.

"I did." Brody conceded that one.

"No shit." Case turned back to Harvey, who'd just returned. The smell of cigarette smoke swirled around him.

One blue-haired lady leapt to her feet and cried out, "Bingo!" She ran to the caller, waving her bingo card.

Brody smiled at her enthusiasm; he couldn't help it. Hell, he'd smiled more in the past few weeks than he'd smiled in the past several years.

He glanced sideways at Mandy. She was smiling, too. Her kind expression warmed his heart. Mandy had such a soft spot for these people. He'd never belonged anywhere, never been part of a close-knit community or a family before. Envy carved a little spot inside him, envy for a life he'd never have. He'd chosen a lonely road and didn't plan on taking a detour.

He turned back to his beer and caught Mandy watching him. "Hey, I'll take another."

She poured another beer, filling the glass and placing it in front of him.

"Thanks."

"See you tomorrow," Case addressed Brody, slapped a five on the counter, and nodded at Harvey. Brody watched him leave and blew out a long, slow breath when the door clicked shut. He leaned back and propped his feet on the bar rail, finally able to relax. Bingo had ended and the karaoke host took the caller's place.

Brody had suffered through karaoke last weekend. He'd heard one blue-hair who thought she was God's greatest gift to classical love songs but couldn't sing one correct note. Another talked the songs because she couldn't sing. Hell, at least Harvey could sing.

He settled in for a long, late summer's night. Oddly enough, he felt at home here more than he had anywhere else in a long time, maybe ever.

A slight grin stretched the corners of his usually grim mouth, and it felt good. Felt right. Across the room, Mandy took a drink order. Her gaze wrapped around him, warming him from the inside out. For a man who never stopped climbing the next mountain, being content didn't exist in his vocabulary; but with her, it did. In some deeply buried part of him, a seed germinated, poked its head through the fresh earth, seeking the sun. Only Brody didn't seek the sun. He hunted down the darkness so that others could have the sun.

It was the way of things.

He'd been tagged to defend all that these people held dear. He couldn't do it hanging around a veterans bar in a small town in the middle of nowhere.

Hell, these people were stuck in a time warp. Most of them didn't lock their doors.

Was that so bad?

Damned if he knew. In less than three months, he'd be back in the Middle East doing what he found comfortable and familiar. The crowd thinned out after bingo. A new, slightly younger crowd trickled in for Monday-night karaoke. The DJ, Harold, older than most of the songs on his outdated CDs, tottered up to the small stage. He picked up the mic and started the music. A second later, Harold launched into an ancient country song, butchering it beyond recognition.

Next to Brody, Harvey thumbed through his collection of karaoke songs and selected a few. Brody ordered another beer and braced himself for a long night. Singer after singer tortured his ears until he swore he'd never be the same.

Harvey walked up to the mic. Brody relaxed slightly. At least Harvey could sing. He crooned a pretty decent rendition of *Desperado,* one of Brody's favorite songs as he fancied himself a bit of a desperado.

Brody glanced up, caught Mandy's eyes and held them. His iron-clad heart cracked, just a hairline fracture, repairable with the proper tools and distance. Only he didn't have either, not tonight. Tonight he couldn't drag his gaze away from Mandy's warm brown eyes, couldn't catch his breath, couldn't think a lucid thought. The song and the woman all melded together with his loneliness and ever-present guilt, fusing them into something new and different.

Like man in a trance, he stood and held his hand out to her, half expecting her rejection. She placed her smaller hand in his big one in a heart-melting display of trust. He wrapped his long fingers around hers and tugged her onto the dance floor. The sparse crowd murmured around them, but he blocked them out. Brody wrapped his arms loosely around her waist and resisted the urge to plaster her against his hungry body; instead he kept a respectful distance between their lower bodies. Mandy looped her arms around his neck. She blinked up at him, enveloped by the same fog which had thickened his senses.

They shuffled around the dance floor, his leg not making him the most coordinated of dancers. He liked her height, liked her curves, liked her. His nostrils filled with her fresh scent. He gripped her tighter, dipped his head low and nuzzled her neck. She gasped, and he drew back, but only a small distance. A few inches separated their lips. Her full mouth fell open, and she ran her pink tongue over her plump lower lip. He bit back a groan. Everywhere she touched him seared his body. His cock stiffened like a good soldier, ready for action. It wouldn't be the only part of him disappointed at the end of the evening.

"This is your song, isn't it?"

More than she'd ever know. He'd never let somebody love him. Never. And his life was a prison created by loneliness. Mandy understood. He knew she did. He saw it in her eyes. Two people afraid to give their hearts, claiming they loved their freedom, when they weren't even fooling themselves.

The song ended too soon, yet not soon enough.

He held onto her, not wanting the moment to end—a foolish line of logic, especially for a man who prided himself on his logic. Mandy gazed up at him as if he held the key to her dreams. For a brief moment, he desperately wanted to be that man, even if it was an illusion. He didn't even hold the key to unlock his own personal hell. She'd never know his demons, and he'd never be her knight in tattered armor or even her one-knight-stand.

Lame, but true.

* * * *

Mandy wrenched her body from Brody's grasp. She shook her head and covered her mouth with her hand. She'd almost kissed him, begged him to kiss her. His brows drew together in a firm, uncompromising line. Those pale blue eyes posted a closed for business sign, especially if that business concerned her.

They'd almost stepped into forbidden territory. Fear slammed into her with brute force and strangled the breath from her lungs.

Oh my God, I can't be falling for another man with a craving for danger and a death wish.

She whipped around and marched to the bar, leaving

Brody standing on the dance floor. A few seconds later, he reclaimed his seat and wrapped his hands around his cold one. The baseball game on the overhead TV caught and held his attention, as if nothing had happened.

Maybe she hadn't rocked his world, but in hers a major earthquake rocked the landscape of her heart. She fought to rearrange it back to a familiar setting, but the lay of the land had altered. Old convictions leaned precariously, ready to be taken out by the next strong wind. Her comfort zone cracked like concrete facades on old buildings and blocked the road ahead. She didn't know whether to turn back or trudge ahead through the rubble.

Behind her lay the comfort of her life with Frank, a nice wallow in the warm mud of self-pity. Ahead lay a hostile land of shattered beliefs and unrealized dreams.

Caro touched her arm, and Mandy jumped. "What are you doing here?"

"Waiting for a drink. This is a bar, isn't it?"

Mandy popped the cork on a bottle of Merlot and poured her friend a glass. "How long have you been here?"

Caro's slow smile said it all. She tapped Mandy on the hand. "Chemistry, my dear. Chemistry."

Mandy closed her eyes and hugged her stomach. "Was it real obvious?" She opened them, one at a time and peeked around the room.

"Only to me because I know you like a sister. He gets to you. Frank was comfortable; you'd known him since grade school. Brody isn't comfortable."

"I don't need another man, especially not one with a life-endangering job. I'm fine with my life as it is." Mandy picked up a tray to bus a few tables.

"You're not even fooling yourself with that statement."

"He'll be gone in a few months. Even if something could happen between us, he's a soldier. I couldn't put myself through that hell again, night after night wondering if I'd hear from him the next day, dying a million deaths with each unrecognized phone call or stranger knocking on my door."

Caro rubbed her chin and nodded sagely. "Maybe he's not the man for you long-term, but what's wrong with short-term? A little sexual healing goes a long way. I highly recommend it."

Mandy said nothing.

Caro reached across the bar and grabbed Mandy's arm when she attempted to walk away. "Frank's dead, honey. You're not. Don't bury your life with his."

Pulling away from Caro, she sauntered past Brody at the end of the bar, forcing her feet into a casual walk. Brody didn't even glance her way, appearing as if Harvey's latest story garnered his utmost attention.

Frustrated, she plunked the dirty glasses on the bar tray and swiped at the table top with a wet rag. She wiped off another table, and another, whether it needed it or not.

Glancing over her shoulder, her gaze clashed with Brody's. A hint of sadness tinged with regret glinted in his blue eyes. He swallowed and wrapped his hands around the beer glass. His mouth pressed into a firm, stubborn line. She looked away, heat spreading to her cheeks, but also southward to that spot between her legs.

She pushed her hair out of her eyes and brushed past Brody. Keeping her back to him, she loaded the dishwasher. Try as she might, she couldn't block out a pair of pale blue eyes.

Chapter 7—Blitz

What the fuck was he doing here?

Brody straightened his shoulders and projected an air of absolute confidence. Fierce, bad-ass soldier that he was, these teenagers scared the crap out of him. He didn't know a damn thing about kids, didn't care to know, and wanted the hell out of here.

Now.

Only his options were limited—be here or somewhere too close to Mandy. He'd avoided her since last night as best as a guy could who lived and worked on her property. He'd started on the house at seven AM, noting she'd made a haphazard attempt to clean it. Knowing she lay sleeping upstairs didn't exactly help his raging hard on and gutter-dwelling imagination. She'd staggered into the kitchen about eleven AM, poured a cup of coffee, and excused herself. A few minutes later, he'd heard the crunch of gravel. At two-thirty, he headed to the football field, grateful to escape the smothering memories of Frank and his own memories of how good Mandy felt in his arms during that slow dance.

Brody glanced at the empty stands, empty except for two older ladies watching him with malice in their eyes like females who ate their young. They scared him more than the teenagers.

Gathered in a small group, the offensive players stared back at him like they expected him to say something wise and profound. Damn, Brody didn't say that kind of crap. He wasn't a fucking inspirational speaker, he was a man of action, a soldier. He sure as hell wasn't a coach.

He didn't dare cuss around these kids, or their mommies and daddies would be all over his ass.

Out of the corner of his eye, he caught Case watching him, expecting him to fuck up, big-time. Well, screw that. Brody always rose to a challenge. Always.

He forced a smile on his lips. It felt tight and unnatural.

Judging by the grimaces on the kids' faces, they thought so, too.

"Uh, so, why don't you tell me who you are and what positions you play?"

Nothing. Absolutely nothing, except they blinked. This was not going well. Case smirked.

Fine, they wanted to be assholes, he'd be one right back. "Which one of you is the starting quarterback?"

They all looked to one tall kid, lanky and angular, like most teenage jocks. The kid stepped forward. "Connor McCoy, Junior. Quarterback. All-league and all-district last season," the kid recited as if giving name, rank, and serial number.

Connor met Brody's direct gaze, and his eyes never wavered. The kid had guts and a cocky confidence, a must-have quality in a quarterback. Brody nodded and jotted some notes on his clipboard. Each kid introduced himself, keeping his answers short and to the point. They regarded him with equal parts of hope and suspicion reflected in their eyes.

When they finished, Connor spoke again. "Your turn." Skepticism crept into his voice.

Fine, he'd give it to them straight. "Brody Jensen. State champion, Wisconsin Triple-A. All-state first-team quarterback. Played one year at Michigan."

Connor didn't look impressed. "One year?"

"Yeah, crappy grades. They booted me out. Guess I wasn't so hot after all."

The kids all exchanged looks. Connor, as spokesman, shrugged one shoulder. "So, are you gonna make us better?"

Brody wasn't sure he could answer that. He never made promises he couldn't keep. "Maybe. How good were you?"

"Made the state semis. This year we want to win it all." Connor's eyes narrowed. He didn't so much as flinch under Brody's dissecting glare. His teammates gathered round their quarterback, obviously ready to jump to his defense.

"Fine, listen up. I don't much like kids. I don't have any

driving ambition to be a coach. But I guarantee you, I know football. I don't like to lose, and if you'll buy in one-hundred percent, we'll make a run at it."

The boys all looked to Connor, waiting for his reaction. He worked his jaw, looked into the distance. The uncomfortable silence stretched into long seconds. Most of the boys shuffled their feet and looked at the ground. Out on the field, the defense ran through their drills. A bug buzzed by and landed on Brody's arm. He smacked it dead.

Finally Connor refocused on Brody and shrugged one shoulder. "We'll see." He made no commitment, but he didn't spit in Brody's face either. He guessed that was a plus.

Brody almost smiled. The kid reminded him of a certain cocky high school player from years ago. He could work with that. He liked the kid, and he liked the solidarity the team showed toward their team captain. They had his back.

"Are your boys ready?" Case called from several yards away.

His boys? Well, crap. The kids stared at him, as if expecting something. "Uh, don't you guys do warm-up exercises or something?"

Connor spiked one eyebrow and scowled at him but didn't move. Brody scowled back, neither of them budging in this battle of wills. Brody didn't blink, didn't waver—fuck, he didn't even breathe. He'd be damned if some snot-nosed kid would get the best of him. But Connor had balls. The kid narrowed his eyes, showing more courage than most men twice his age. With all his buddies gathered around to shore him up, Connor stood his ground, refusing to back down and lose face. Brody understood the mind of a teenage boy and racked his brains to come up with workable solution that would save face for both of them.

"Offense! Get your butts over here. NOW!" Case bellowed from the middle of the field, effectively providing the solution Brody needed. "What're you doing, Con? Knitting sweaters?"

Connor gave a guilty start. "Coming, Coach." With a heavy sigh, he gestured to his teammates to follow him.

"Fucking idiot," Connor said to his friend as they walked by, loud enough for Brody to hear him. As a unit, they jogged out to the middle of the field and started their warm-ups.

Brody stood on the sidelines, totally out of his element, and feeling like the idiot his players believed he was.

* * * *

Mandy glanced up every time she heard the door open. Uncertainty gnawed at her heart even as she blockaded her emotions safely behind the dam. Yet, the dam sprang the occasional leak, and she didn't like it one bit. Dancing with a desperado didn't help matters. At the thought of a certain blue-eyed man, her gaze swung back to the door.

She'd avoided Brody all day, but now, as unreasonable as it seemed, she wanted him to come in the bar. He'd woken her early in the morning with his incessant pounding as he worked on the house. He'd come back from town with a load of supplies. Later a lumber truck showed up with even more. She didn't ask him what it cost, didn't want to know, but she'd find a way to pay him back before he left.

According to Case, Brody had shown up at practice, but her brother wasn't forthcoming with any more information than that.

The door opened again, followed by the thump-thump of Brody's cane.

Forcing her body to behave, Mandy poured three beers from the tap for a table of regulars. She didn't look up, even when she sensed Brody sitting on his barstool a few feet from her. "The usual?"

"Yeah." His voice dipped low.

She plucked another glass from the shelf and held it under the tap, filling it to the rim. Only when she placed it on the counter did she look up and straight into his weary blue gaze.

He clutched the glass and raised it to his lips, watching her over the rim. If only she read minds.

"How'd your first day of coaching go?"

"Pretty rough." His self-deprecating smile warmed her heart.

"The kids wear you out?" She leaned against the opposite counter and straightened her apron, smoothing out the wrinkles.

"Something like that. When did I get to be so old?" One corner of his mouth quirked, showing off a dimple so out of place on a rugged face like his.

"I often wonder that myself." She filled a tray with drinks as she talked. "Go easy on them. They've had a tough time of it. Their head coach got fired a week ago. Case took over. My brother's a great defensive coach, but the old coach's absence left the offense orphaned."

"Fired?" Brody shifted in his seat.

Mandy cleared her throat. "Seems he got caught fixing grades for some of his players. The new principal fired him. The team and a lot of people in this town thought the punishment was too harsh. He'd done a lot for the football program, and the team adored him."

"That explains why they look at me like I'm the second coming of Satan."

She laughed, unable to help herself. "He's a tough act to follow when it comes to coaching football. At least he's no longer on the island. That'd make things even more difficult." Mandy knelt down for a bottle of wine from the refrigerator. The whole deal made her sick to her stomach. She hurt for her brother and for the kids.

Brody raked his hand through his hair. "Well, crap."

"The whole town put big expectations on the team to make State finals this year. They came within a game last year, and pretty much the entire team's back."

"How come nobody told me all this at your mom's house?"

"We didn't know. I just got the scoop from Caro. She heard it from the principal's assistant." Mandy hoisted the tray onto the palm of one hand and walked off. She felt his blue eyes drill into her backside. She straightened her spine and walked with a spring in her step.

Mandy doled out the tray of drinks to a couple different tables without spilling a drop. When she turned back to the bar, Brody's gaze dropped. He fiddled with the cardboard coaster. Harvey slid onto the barstool next to him, his jaws flapping.

Mandy counted out ten dollars' worth of pull tabs for one of her regulars.

"Hey, I'll have another." Brody's husky voice shot a tremor of desire from her toes all the way to her head, then circled back around to pool between her legs.

Mandy poured another beer. When she placed it in front of him, he reached for it at the same time. Their fingers grazed each other. Brody stroked her knuckles with the tip of a calloused finger. One simple, gentle stroke, and yet her body purred like a contented kitten.

She staggered back a step, her fingers flying to her mouth. "I—I—" Her stammered words didn't link into a coherent sentence.

"I'm no good at this," Brody said quietly.

"This?" she stuttered. Mandy fumbled for a bottle of tequila and almost dropped it.

"Football. Coaching."

Mandy tried to relax. "Give yourself a chance. I'm sure you'll get the hang of it."

"I guess we'll see." He raised one eyebrow, as if she wasn't fooling him. This wasn't about football.

"There's nothing to see. It is what it is. You're the best man for the job."

He scowled. The muscle ticked in his jaw. "Don't kid yourself. I'm not. I don't put down roots."

"No one's asking you to stay for more than a few months."

Mandy threw some ice, tequila, and margarita mix in a blender, and punched the button. The noise didn't drown out the conflicting conversations in her head.

Brody leaned forward, elbows on the bar, chin resting on his hands. "I don't like kids."

"You said that."

"Want to make sure I get my point across."

"You're getting your point across—no kids, no animals, no roots, no relationships. Got it." Her voice carried across the room and a few customers turned in their seats to look at her. She ignored them.

Brody cocked his head to one side and rested his hands on the edge of the bar. "I'm glad you understand. I can't leave much room for misinterpretation." Mandy's chest tightened, pressing hard on her rib cage and making it difficult to breathe. She popped the tops off a couple beers and counted out another ten dollars in pull tabs. Skirting around the bar, she left him hunched over the counter, deep in thought or fighting his own demons. Not that it mattered because to her, it was all the same.

She lived that story.

* * * *

A deep hoarse shout woke Mandy out of a sound sleep. She shot up in bed and knocked Marlin off the pillow next to her. Flipping on the nightstand light, she darted a glance around the room. The cat shot an indignant glare over his shoulder and stalked off.

Mandy's heart thudded in her chest. She'd heard cries like that before from Frank, but he never talked about whatever haunted him. Guys like him never did.

She clutched her nightgown to her chest and listened.

"No, no, no! Watch out! Agh!" Distressed shouts mingled with words of alarm, some as clear as day, while others were unintelligible.

Shooting to her feet, Mandy grabbed a robe and ran down the stairs. She didn't stop to think of the consequences. Brody needed her. It'd been a long time since someone needed her; she'd been the one doing the needing for so long.

Mandy wrenched open the unlocked door and entered the dimly lit guest room. With shaking hands, she flipped on a small lamp near the door.

Across the room, Brody tossed and turned on the bed, gripping the blanket, every muscle in his body tense and coiled for action. Sweat poured down his forehead and drenched his dark hair. He squeezed his eyes shut as he struggled with an imagined enemy.

She approached with caution, as memories of a distressed Frank flooded back to her.

"Brody?"

No response. He'd gone too deep inside some living hell. She shuddered to think of the things he'd seen. That Frank had seen. Those horrors so many returning servicemen endured every single day. Her heart went out to him, and she'd take his pain as her own if she could.

"Brody!" She raised her voice and touched his shoulder, gently shaking him. Experience warned her not to get too close until he was fully awake, but her driving desire to help him overrode her caution. He stiffened under her touch but didn't wake. She shook harder. "Brody!"

His entire body convulsed as he shouted words in a language she didn't understand. Before she could jump clear, he shot up in bed and grabbed her arms. Throwing her onto her back on the mattress, he pinned her underneath him with his body—his very naked upper body. Mandy held still, afraid to struggle.

"Brody?"

He stared down at her, his blue eyes not seeing her but some imagined enemy. His chest heaved and beads of sweat dripped off his body onto her T-shirt.

"Brody?" She forced the fear from her voice, kept it

steady and calm. His body shook as he gripped her arms tighter. "Brody!" she yelled his name this time as panic built inside her. He could snap her neck easily with his big hands and not wake until it was too late. "Brody! Wake up. You're having a bad dream."

His grip on her arms loosened and his eyes refocused on her face. Brody blinked several times and shook his head several times as if to clear it.

"Oh, crap." Releasing her, he rolled off her and sat on the edge of the bed. He scrubbed his face with his hands then buried his face in them. "I'm—I'm sorry," he said, his voice muffled.

She hated to see him so vulnerable and confused. It broke her heart.

"Brody. You okay?" She sat up and reached for him. He turned, wrapped his arms around her, and clung to her as if she and only she kept the mad dogs at bay.

He wasn't fully awake or none of this would be happening. With his face buried in her hair, his warm breath tickled her neck. His lips touched the sensitive skin below her earlobe. Wrapping her arms tight around him, she pressed her cheek against his cold, clammy one.

Memories flooded back of other times, other nights, of Frank's rapid, shallow breathing, his shaking body in a cold sweat, the terror in his eyes—another person, another place in time. Yet life had a habit of circling around, and it'd circled back on her.

Caro often declared life presented you with the same problems until you learned to deal with them. If that were true, Mandy hadn't learned a darn thing.

Brody's body shuddered from some repressed memory. She understood a soldier's mind to a point, especially Special Forces guys. They were masters at compartmentalizing. In fact, the military chose men with that very quality. Unfortunately, no matter how secure the cell in which you jailed your demons, they always managed to scratch and claw their way out.

Brody moaned, sounding like the wounded coyote she'd found on her doorstep years ago. He gripped her tighter. Mandy held the back of his head, caressing his scalp with her fingers. Their cheeks and bodies pressed tightly together under the cloak of the night. He turned his mouth toward hers, as if seeking comfort, a comfort she could give him.

Despite every argument against it, she slid her lips along his rough cheek and angled her head, just so. He didn't wait for an engraved invitation but RSVP'd with his mouth. It wasn't a gentle kiss or a wild kiss, but something in between, something hungry yet tentative, seeking and finding. All those days of wanting him but denying it had built up to this, and she wanted him with a need both overwhelming and all-consuming, to hell with guilt and regret. She'd deal with that later.

Brody's lips tasted of mint toothpaste mixed with the salt from his sweat. He tasted of man; hard, uncompromising man, the best kind. At least for her.

Mandy parted her lips. His tongue slipped inside and danced with hers, a slow waltz between two wounded yet consenting adults. He cupped her face in his hands, deepened the kiss, upped the tempo of the dance to a sultry tango. Her brain exited her body, spinning out of the room and taking with it the last of her coherent thoughts.

He gently pushed her down onto the bed and angled his body on top of hers, as he demanded more from her kisses. One of his hands slid under her nightshirt, along the side of her ribcage, coming to a stop at the curve of her breast.

Mandy wrapped one leg around his. The man slept in sweats, which she found decidedly odd, especially considering how warm the nights still were. But his impressive chest was bare and, God, she loved his chest.

Using her body, she begged him to touch her and ease some of their mutual pain. Just for a moment she wanted to feel whole again. She arched her back and pressed her hips into his, rubbing against his hard erection.

"I fucking want you," he whispered against her mouth.

"I want you, too," she panted as she slid her hands along the muscles bulging in his strong arms.

"You're so fucking hot, I want—" He stopped in midsentence as a doggie tongue lashed at her face and Brody's. Startled, they broke the kiss instantly. Brody rolled off her and onto the side of the bed in one quick, surprisingly graceful movement. Sunny stood on the bed, tail wagging his entire hind end. He dropped a wet, slimy ball between then and waited expectantly, every muscle in his body poised for the chase.

Fully awake and fully back to her senses, Mandy scrambled off the bed and stood, hugging her body. Yanking down her T-shirt, she squinted at him in the dim light. Deep worry lines cut across Brody's weary face.

"Oh, man." He raked his fingers through his mussed up hair and ran a hand over his face. He lifted his head, his eyes full of anguish. "I'm sorry."

"I—need to go now." Mandy ran out of the room and back to the safety of her bedroom. She leaned against the closed door, put her head in her hands, and let the tears roll down her cheeks.

She didn't know if she was crying for herself, Frank, or Brody. Conflicting emotions jumbled together leaving her weak and drained. She sank to the floor and cried until she fell asleep curled in a little ball, alone with her dreams, disturbing images of Frank dissolving to Brody's face until she couldn't make out Frank's features anymore and only Brody's stood out sharp and crisp.

Chapter 8—Wounded

Out on the field, Sunset Harbor High School's finest ran a warm-up lap with Connor in the lead. The kid reminded Brody of a certain headstrong quarterback from years ago. Unfortunately, Brody had allowed his stubborn ego to run the show just as Connor appeared to be doing right now.

Brody raked a hand through his hair, out of his element and frustrated. Coaching wasn't his thing. Nor did he care to be working with kids, watching his language, or dodging pointed questions from parents about how much playing time their sons would get. Thank God that last question he deferred to the head coach. Let the bastard take some of the heat. Case didn't lift a finger to offer suggestions on the opposing teams or give advice on how best to handle teenage boys. Instead, he observed Brody like a spy gathering intel on the enemy. Brody shouldn't be the enemy.

Connor, Case, and the team weren't his only issue. Mandy ranked at the top of his solutions-needed list.

This morning, he'd dragged himself out of bed at dawn and walked along the beach until he'd found an old bench partially hidden by the trees. He sat down and worked on new plays for Friday night's home opener and studied the unfamiliar playbook.

Any idiot could guess he was mostly running from Mandy, which pissed him off. He'd never run from anything in his life. Until now.

He couldn't face her after last night. Shame flooded through him, shame for being weak enough to have nightmares in the first place and more shame for taking advantage of her sympathy. She'd responded to him with unrestrained enthusiasm and a sparkle in her eyes solely for him. He'd done a slow burn all night thinking about how her body felt against his. Her full lips against his mouth left an imprint on his brain which still hadn't faded. Her pretty face was tattooed on the inside of his eyelids when he closed his eyes.

Ah, man, this wasn't good. Not at all. He could deal with his attraction to her. But the way she'd looked at him—God help him.

The last thing he needed was for his buddy's widow to fall in love with a guy who couldn't put down roots, had to be constantly stimulated by danger, and never wanted to be tied down by a family. Besides, Brody was convenient, and Mandy was vulnerable. Her attraction had nothing to do with who he was or wasn't. Even worse, on some level, she'd picked another Frank. She didn't need another Frank.

If it hadn't been for that stupid-assed blind dog, they'd have screwed each other's brains out. He'd never forgive himself if that happened. Never. He needed to find her a more suitable man and fast before their shared loneliness overrode their common sense.

At least Mandy worked a lot—four nights at the bar and serving the lunch crowd during the week at the Country Kettle Cafe. Immersing herself in work was one way to avoid dealing with her problems. He used the tactic himself.

Like right now, for instance.

In some ways, he was grateful for this coaching job. He needed a distraction. Working on the house gave him way too much time to think. At least he could target his razor-sharp focus on football, rather than his buddy's widow.

"Mr. Jensen? Hey, Mr. Jensen?" Connor snapped his fingers in front of Brody's face, slamming Brody back to the present.

The kid refused to call Brody *Coach* and his teammates followed suit. Brody hated being *Mr. Jensen*, but his hardass quarterback obviously figured he'd need to earn the title first. Brody would be damned if he'd force the kid.

"Yeah, what?" Brody mentally kicked himself for letting his attention waver.

Connor studied him as if assessing his adversary for weaknesses like any good warrior. "You've got company." He hooked a thumb in the direction of the bleachers.

Brody's eyes tracked instantly to his *company*. Mandy gave him a small wave from her seat on the second row of bleachers, a few seats from all the mothers and grandmothers who liked to hang out at football practice, watch their kids, gossip, and knit.

Brody turned to Connor. "Lead the offense on a lap around the field."

"We just ran a lap." The kid dug in his heels and didn't budge, throwing the challenge in Brody's face.

"Fine. Two laps."

"You're just saying that 'cause you wanna flirt with Aunt Mandy."

Aunt Mandy? "Three laps. Actually, let's make it four 'cause I'm a generous guy."

Connor opened his mouth to protest then clamped it shut. His brown eyes narrowed to angry slits.

"Just keep talking, kid. You'll be the most unpopular guy on the offense."

Connor's eyes flashed with anger, the most emotion Brody had seen out of him.

Brody glanced at his watch then back at Connor. "You're not back yet?" He added some steel to his voice so the kid would know he meant business and had had enough of his bullshit. "Get out there *now*."

Connor didn't wait around for another lap to be tacked on—he took off at a run.

Brody walked to the bleachers, inclined his head at the knitting club. He was winning them over. Today, they tittered like a group of hens over a new rooster in the hen house. He wished he could win the team over as easily as he'd won them over. But then, he'd always been good with the ladies.

He couldn't stop the slow smile from spilling across his face as he turned his attention to Mandy. "Hey."

"Hi." She looked at him through lowered lashes in a shy yet sexy way that sent his foolish heart thumping in his chest.

"I'm surprised to see you." He shifted his weight from one

foot to the other, uncomfortable under the scrutiny of the ladies two rows up.

"You left this on the kitchen counter." She held up his wallet.

"Thanks." He reached for it, and his thumb grazed hers. Such a simple act yet the intensity of the contact almost drove him to his knees. "I—I have to get back to the guys. Are you going to stick around?"

"I thought I would until I have to go to work in an hour. If you don't mind."

Mind? Hell, yeah, but hell, no, too. She'd distract the heck out of him, but he didn't want her to go either.

"You might want to get back to your boys."

"Uh, yeah, okay." Embarrassed, he hurried across the field as fast as he could on one good leg.

First things first. He'd take charge of the offense and show these kids he knew football, even if he didn't know how to coach it.

Connor finished his laps and stood near the center of the field, his angry eyes on Brody as he talked with his buddies. Brody cupped his hands over his mouth and yelled for Connor to come to the sidelines. Connor jogged over, his face an unreadable mask. The kid rarely gave anything away, except for his displeasure with Brody as coach.

"Yeah?" Connor balanced on the balls of his feet, all restless energy, chest heaving from his run. He glanced over his shoulder, eager to get back to his guys. He gave his coach only half his attention, as if not buying Brody had anything useful to say. He might be right about that, but Connor didn't get a vote. Not anymore.

For the past two days, Brody watched the offense. He let Connor take over and lead the team while Brody contented himself with observing and taking notes. Case didn't interfere, but the disapproving scowl on his face said it all.

"I want to see progression drills." Brody locked gazes with Connor. He'd pussy-footed around this surly teenager enough; time to bring out the big guns. Connor didn't stand a chance against an adult male with tons of training and experience in the art of mental warfare.

"We never do those drills. I don't need it." The gutsy kid's gaze didn't waver.

"Really? You don't need to practice making the best passing decisions on the field? You've got it all figured out?"

Connor's gaze wavered, along with his certainty. "I've been starting quarterback for two years."

"You don't think NFL quarterbacks do this drill?"

"I don't know." Connor looked down and shuffled his feet.

"Well, guess what, Mr. Expert. They do."

Connor lifted his head. "How the hell would you know?"

"And how would you know what I do or don't know?"

Brody had him, and Connor knew it. Without another word, he headed back to the field where his teammates waited. Brody hobbled after him.

A warm of layer of satisfaction settled over him. He could do this. Maybe it wasn't so hard after all. They were just a bunch of damn kids.

He drilled them on the same set of exercises for several minutes, evaluating their reactions, shouting suggestions, and making notes. All the while, Mandy's gaze burned into his back. In a moment of weakness, he looked over his shoulder and caught her eye. There went that stupid smile again. He couldn't seem to control it.

"Shouldn't you be watching the team instead of my sister?" Case moved to stand beside him, his face tight with dislike.

Guilty as charged. Flexing the fingers of one hand, Brody ignored Case and barked some instructions to the first-team offense.

"Connor hates progression drills. The old coach never made him do them."

Brody didn't reply.

Connor zeroed in on one receiver and threw an interception. Meanwhile, his wide-open tight end waved his arms and all but ran a flag up the flagpole to get his attention. "He gets by on raw talents, but the basics aren't there."

"He's done okay in the past."

"He can be better, so much better. One, he's not reading the coverage." Brody ticked off the points on his fingers. "Two, he doesn't run through his checkdowns. Three, he has a couple favorite receivers, and he tries to force it, and four, he thinks he knows more than the coach."

"Good luck with that last one. In fact, all of them. The kid is good enough to take this team to the top of the heap. Maybe we don't need all that other crap to muddy the waters."

"He could play college ball and what he's doing isn't good enough for a D-1 college."

"This is a little school on an island in the middle of nowhere. He'll be lucky to get a community college scholarship. Why mess with what's worked for him in the past? It's good enough to get us to the championships."

"If you know all the answers, what the hell do you need me for?"

"I'm not sure I do." Case walked off without another word, leaving Brody to stew over the other man's lack of support.

Brody blew his whistle and motioned the offense over to him. They kneeled around him in a semi-circle as he outlined a couple new plays he'd added to the playbook.

"That play will never work." Connor rose to his feet and nodded to his teammates for confirmation. They bobbed their heads, one hundred percent behind their quarterback.

"Why not?" Brody challenged the kid.

"'Cause you don't know the Tigers defense like we do."

"So you've watched them practice this year?"

Connor hesitated. "No, I, uh. No."

"Well, I saw them on Monday afternoon. Took the ferry to the mainland and watched them. I'm convinced this running play will exploit a weakness I saw in their line."

Connor didn't like being called out in front of his buddies. If looks could kill, Brody would be hanging from the goalpost right about now. Several pairs of eyes moved from the quarterback to the coach and back again.

Tired of arguing with the kid, Brody dismissed him with a wave of his hand. "Get back out on the field and let's run through these new plays."

Connor didn't move. The rest of his teammates took their cue from their quarterback and hesitated. Brody half expected Connor to flip him the finger and walk off the field. Attitude radiated from him like heat on the desert on a hundred-and-twenty-degree day.

"What are you guys waiting for? Move it." Brody raised his voice to drill sergeant level. The boys jumped off Connor's sinking ship and high-tailed it back to the field.

"You have a question, Connor?"

Shrugging, Connor swung his gaze to his disloyal buddies. With a pissy sigh, he sprinted after his teammates.

Brody released his held breath. He'd never bargained on a group of teenagers being so hard to handle. He had his work cut out for him and then some, both here and elsewhere. He glanced toward Mandy, craving a friendly smile, but the bleachers were empty.

The lead weight of disappointment settled in his stomach.

* * * *

Mandy glanced at the clock, yawning and trying to pry open her eyes. She flung her arms to the sides and groaned. What the heck was she thinking? The clock read six AM. No sane person got up this early.

She stared at the ceiling in the semi-darkness. Early morning sunlight peeked through the slats in her blinds. A stray bird or two sang outside her window along with a cricket's peaceful chirping. Nothing should sound so cheerful this early in the morning.

Mandy sat on the edge of the bed and rubbed her eyes.

Brody didn't come into the bar last night. Mandy tamped down the bitter taste of disappointment, telling herself his absence was for the best. Ever since their mutual lonely hearts club makeout session, he'd avoided her, and she'd been more than happy to avoid him back.

Regardless, the coward wasn't getting out of their morning walk. He'd started these forced marches, and she didn't intend on letting him off the hook just because the man evaded emotional issues. So they'd had a moment of stupidity and indulged themselves. Big deal, it didn't mean any more to her than it did to him.

After pulling on a pair of sweats and a T-shirt, Mandy dug under the bed for her shoes. Marlin watched her with one eye from his place on the other pillow. Sunny rolled over on his dog bed and kept his back to her. Her animals were smarter than she was.

Putting a couple bottles of water in a small pack, she left the house, glancing back toward the guest room. It appeared dark, not a light on. A wicked smile crossed her face. Payback was a bitch.

Mandy pounded on his door. "Rise and shine, sleepyhead."

No answer. His SUV was parked in the driveway, as usual. Maybe he'd left without her. She pounded again. Inside she heard thumping sounds and a muffled curse. The door slammed open.

Brody stood in the doorway, shirtless with his sweats low on his hips. He squinted down at her and yawned.

"You're late." She grinned at him, thoroughly enjoying their role reversal.

"What time is it?" He rubbed his eyes and glanced behind him at a clock on the wall. He stretched, accentuating every one of his abs and his flat stomach. Her gaze followed the trail of dark hair to the waistband of his sweats. Clearing her throat, she forced her gaze back to his face. He caught her looking at him, but his hooded eyes gave nothing away. Grabbing a neatly folded T-shirt out of a nearby drawer, he pulled it over his head then sat on the edge of the bed and pulled on his shoes and socks. She couldn't help but admire how his biceps flexed as he did this simple task.

"Ready?" Her voice sounded a little hoarse so she cleared her throat.

"Yup." He shut the door and stood beside her, all six-feet-two of him. His body might not be perfect anymore, but she didn't sweat the small stuff. It was close enough to make her mouth water. He'd certainly yanked her sex drive out of hibernation.

At first after Frank died, she'd sworn she'd never marry again. She'd be like her mother and aunt, content to live her life without a man in it. Only they'd lost their husbands much later in life, after they'd had a chance to raise a family and spend decades together. She'd never had that chance, and she wanted that second chance.

Part of her felt anger at Frank for insisting on such a dangerous career, even when she'd begged him to make each mission his last. Yet there had always been another mission until the one that had taken his life.

They walked along the dirt road, lost in thought, even though Mandy couldn't shake her awareness of the very virile man next to her.

Finally, Brody broke the silence between them. "I'm sorry about the other night. It shouldn't have happened."

"But it did. Don't be so hard on yourself, Brody. We're two lonely adults seeking comfort. What happened shouldn't have surprised us."

"Well, it can't happen again."

"No, it can't. " She chanced a glance at him. He stared straight ahead, his face a tense mask.

"I'm leaving at the end of three months."

"I know."

"As soon as the house is done."

"By the way, you've done a great job already."

"Thanks. It'd help if I didn't have to waste my time cleaning up your messes every morning before I started work." A smile tugged at his mouth.

"Sorry. I'm more casual than you about tidiness." She bit back a smile; leave it to Mr. Clean to point out her lack of attention to detail. She'd never admit to him that she actually thought the place was tidy. At least for her standards, obviously not his.

"You call that casual? I call it the aftermath of a ransacking." He slanted her one of his sexy, boyish grins, the kind that melted a woman's heart on contact.

Mandy laughed, unable to mount a comeback. Her bedroom did look like it'd been burglarized with clothes thrown everywhere, drawers open, stuff laying all over the dresser. "How about you pick up a little when we get back before I start in the kitchen?"

"Okay." She hated cleaning the kitchen, as much as she hated cleaning bathrooms.

"I mean it." His stern sergeant's voice didn't work on her.

"Whatever." She studied him and opened her mouth before thinking. "How often do you have nightmares?"

"Not often." A muscle jerked in his jaw.

"Have you gotten treatment?"

"Yeah, I go a couple times a month to see someone. It's getting better. Doesn't happen nearly as much now as it once did."

"Do you have PTSD?"

"Anyone who's seen what I have has some level of trauma, or that person wouldn't be human. I'm better off than most. Just little things, like the occasional nightmare. I don't sit with my back to doors. That kind of crap. It's under control."

She could tell by the expression on his face, he wasn't telling her something. She held her tongue for now. They lapsed into another silence, this one more relaxed. After several more minutes of walking, Mandy turned to Brody, "We should go back now."

Brody didn't answer. In fact, he stumbled a little and stopped as if disoriented. Sweat poured off his face. Mandy touched his arm. He felt cold and clammy. She fought back panic. Was he having a heart attack?

"Brody. What's wrong?"

He sat down on a large rock, his eyes unfocused. His hands shook. Sweat soaked his T-shirt. His face turned grayer than an overcast day. He shook his head and muttered, "Stupid, stupid, stupid."

Mandy fought back the rising fear. "Are you having chest pains?"

"It's not that. It's my leg. This happens sometimes. It's cramping. It'll be okay in a few minutes." His face contorted from the pain.

"Are you sure?" She studied him with concern.

He stared at his hands. "Yeah, I need to get over myself."

She smiled. "Yeah, you do. You're not the only person on earth with an injury."

He took her hand. "Thanks for being here."

She squeezed his hand tight. "I'm glad I was."

He swallowed. "We should head back."

"Are you sure you can walk? It's a long way."

"Of course I am." Releasing her hand, he rose to his feet, limped a few steps, and fell to his knees. Mandy ran to his side, helped him up, and guided him back to the rock.

"I'll get the car."

"I can walk." He tried to smile but grimaced instead.

"Sorry." Mandy shook her head at the pigheaded man. Brody needed to get over himself. Mandy's heart went out to proud, stubborn Brody, a man who wouldn't ask for help even when he needed it most.

Just like her.

Chapter 9—Fanning the Flames

Sometimes life just sucked.

Brody drank half of the glass of ice water in one long gulp as he sat on his usual barstool in the Veterans' Club. Damn, the cool liquid felt good going down—about the only damn thing that did feel good today.

All in all, it'd been a crappy day all around starting with his incident this AM, being picked up by Case, not feeling like working on the house, and then a shitty practice.

Connor fought him every step of the way and resented Brody's guidance as usual. Brody didn't give a shit; he was in charge, not some snot-nosed kid with a chip on his shoulder.

Caro refilled the glass and handed it back to him. "Thirsty?"

"It was hot out there at practice today." Brody managed a tired smile.

"Ready for tomorrow night's home opener?"

"Ready as I'll ever be." Which wasn't very ready at all.

"My nephew is having withdrawals. This'll be his first game without Coach Randle."

"Your nephew?" Brody's head snapped up. This was the first he'd heard about Caro having a relative on the team. Not that it should surprise him; practically every local on this island seemed to be related in some way.

"Connor. You know, the one who throws the ball." Caro made a throwing motion with her arm, as if he was too stupid to figure it out any other way.

"Connor is related to you?" Sure, Connor looked of Native American descent, but he'd never put the two of them together.

"I'm his aunt, sister, mother, and father all rolled into one messy package." She grinned as if relishing the job, and Brody bet that she did.

"No parents?"

"Not that come around. My sister ran off with some rodeo

cowboy a couple years ago. Connor gets a postcard from her once in a while. His worthless father didn't want to pay child support on three different kids so he took off for Alaska."

"Is he always so surly or is it just me?"

Caro laughed, as if she found his question amusing. "Actually, it's just you. He thinks you're a prick and out to get him."

Brody chuckled at the woman's blunt honesty. "I am a prick. But out to get him? No. Not at all. I have my way of doing things. He needs to adjust, especially if he plans on playing in college."

"There won't be any college." Caro looked away, suddenly interested in polishing the bar counter until it shined. He'd hit a nerve.

"Why not? Are his grades bad?"

"They're average, not good enough for any academic help, and God knows, we don't have the money."

"What about a football scholarship?"

Caro frowned at Brody as if he'd lost his fucking mind. "He's not good enough. Don't go filling his mind with that kind of BS."

"I think he's good enough. In fact, I think he's incredibly talented, just undisciplined raw talent."

"Coach Randle told us not to get our hopes up."

"I think *Mr.* Randle is wrong. If he'd only listen to me, I think we can make him a premier high school quarterback."

"Even if he was wrong, you'll be gone at the end of the season. Where does that leave him next year when he needs you the most?"

Brody couldn't make promises he couldn't keep. "I—I—"

"Yeah, back to square one, hotshot. Don't fill his mind with hopes and dreams you can't deliver on."

"We all need hopes and dreams," Brody said quietly.

"Yes, we do. What are yours?" She threw his statement right back in his face. He should've seen it coming.

"I'm living my dream. I travel the world and help root out evil." He squirmed under Caro's assessing stare, knowing she saw right through his bullshit.

"Such a lofty goal must tire a man, make him long for simpler things."

Brody veered down a side road, leaving this conversation behind, and lowered his voice. "I need your help."

"Finding simpler things?"

He glanced around. Convinced no one could hear him, he leaned forward. "With Mandy. I think she's attracted to me."

"And this is a problem? Both of you could use a little romance in your lives."

"That's the last complication I need. She's in love with Frank, not me. I remind her of Frank. None of this has anything to do with how she feels about me except as a replacement for the man she lost. Look, I'm not sticking around. We all know that."

Caro gave him one of those looks that insinuated she knew more than he did. "If you say so."

"Besides, I'm all wrong for her. She needs a nice guy, one who'll be home every night, be a husband and a father, one who'll be there when she needs him. I'm not that guy."

"You could be. What if destiny says you are?"

Brody sighed and wondered how the hell he could get through to this woman. "I could use your help."

"You're doing a damn good job of screwing this up all on your own." She slid a beer to him, foam running over the top and sliding down the sides to circle the bottom of the glass.

"We need to find her a suitable man."

"Maybe we have." Caro's pointed stare left him sputtering.

"No, not me. Don't you get it? What about that guy over there? He comes in here once in a while, seems like a nice guy. I understand he manages the produce section at the grocery store."

"You've been doing your research."

"Not really." He happened to be a good listener and picked up bits and pieces in the bar.

"Then you probably don't know that he's never been married and still lives with his mother."

"Oh." Nope, Brody didn't know that. The guy had to be in his late thirties or early forties. Brody didn't understand a guy living with his mother any longer than necessary. Hell, he'd moved out of his parents' house the day he turned eighteen and never looked back.

"But I'm sure we could dredge up a few possibilities for Mandy if that's what you really want."

"Of course that's what I want. I'm—"

"—leaving. I know. If you say it enough, you might convince yourself." Caro tossed back her long, black hair and patted him on the shoulder. "You should slow down on your drinking." She indicated the half-full glass.

"What? You put so much head on it that I only got half a glass."

Caro's laughter floated back to him as she glided across the room to wait on other customers.

Frustrated, Brody stared down at his beer and the puddle surrounding it. At least Caro had agreed to help him. Or so he thought.

You never could tell with that woman.

* * * *

Caro Phillips considered herself a bit of a magician/healer, or shaman as her people called it. Over the years, she'd been the catalyst by which her eighty-year-old nana met and married the eighty-five-year-old love of her life. They lived happily ever after in a single-wide in Arizona, playing pinochle all day with the "old people." Getting Brody and Mandy together would take all her skills. Her friend struggled with getting involved with another man in a dangerous career. While Caro understood her fears, she considered it bullshit. No benevolent god or great spirit or whatever a person happened to worship would banish a person as good and young as Mandy from her destiny. And Brody, he avoided roots or deep relationships, and wrapped his pain in a suit of Kevlar.

Well, he'd come to the right place. Repairing wounded souls just happened to be Caro's specialty.

Brody might not know what he wanted, but Caro did. Oh, yes, she did. In fact, she knew what they both wanted and needed. She'd play matchmaker for Mandy and some other guy because it'd bring out the green-eyed monster in Brody. The poor guy wouldn't know what hit him, but Caro would. She just needed a little bit of her nana's Salish magic and a lot of luck.

Now to lay the trap for Mandy. First things first, she'd tip over the first domino and steer the rest in the right direction.

Checking her watch, Caro sent Brody to pick up a pizza from the bar down the block. A couple minutes later Mandy walked in. Immediately, her friend scanned the bar for someone then her face fell.

Caro counted her till and feigned ignorance, while watching Mandy from the corner of her eyes. Her gaze kept skipping to the door.

Caro moved in like a lioness stalking her prey. "Looking for someone?"

Mandy gave a guilty start and hurried to wipe a clean counter.

"So how's it going with your hunkalicious carpenter?"

"It's not going. He's just a friend." The door opened and Mandy's gaze snapped to it. When Harvey walked in, disappointment spread across her face. She was so easy to read.

"He'll be right back. He went to pick up a pizza."

"I'm not looking for Brody." The counter practically glowed as Mandy polished harder.

"If you're not looking for him, how did you know who I

was talking about?"

"I just—just need to talk to him about some work on the house."

"My nephew says the sparks between Brody and you would light up the entire town."

Mandy's face turned redder than the new stop sign on Main Street. "Your nephew's a teenager. His hormones are running wild so he thinks everything has to do with sex."

"Is that so?"

"He reads too much into it."

"You were at practice yesterday, right?"

"Brody left his wallet on the counter. I didn't want him to get a ticket." Mandy's threatening glare hit Caro and bounced right off.

"You're so transparent you should be Plexiglas." Caro leaned closer. "Your face is fire engine red."

"It's hot in here."

"Take a deep breath." Caro jerked her chin in the direction of the door. "It's about to get hotter, honey."

Brody nodded to a couple people as he limped to his barstool, balancing a pizza box in one hand. He took his seat. Flustered, Mandy knocked over several bottles of booze, luckily not breaking any.

"Are you okay?" Brody studied Mandy's face.

"It's so hot in here." Mandy fumbled with the bottles, straightening them with shaking hands.

"Really hot." Caro resisted the urge to roll her eyes. Officially off shift, she poured a glass of beer for herself and sat next to Brody.

Sorry, honey, you don't get a vote. I'm taking over and setting fire to your boring life.

Rick, a decent single guy, not Brody's caliber but drop-dead boring, walked to the bar for another beer. Caro pounced. "Rick, are you going to Saturday night's seventies dance?"

"I hadn't given it much thought, but if you're asking." He stared at Caro as if he couldn't believe his good luck. *Down boy, wrong woman.* He was just too average for Caro.

"I'm asking for a single friend. She's got the hots for you."

Brody shot Caro a quick look, and she bit back a smirk. His lips pressed into a firm, hard line, yet he tried so damn hard to look nonchalant. This might be easier than planned.

"She has the hots for me?" Rick shook his head, probably never having heard those words directed at him.

"Yes, you, tiger. How about it, will you be here?" Caro ran a hand over his skinny arm and smiled her best feral smile. It worked. He'd follow her anywhere.

He nodded, never taking his lovesick eyes off her. "Wouldn't miss it for the world."

"Good, we'll save a seat at our table. Won't we, Brody?"

Brody snapped to attention, coming back from wherever his mind had gone for a moment. "Uh, yeah. We'll do that."

"It's settled. See you Saturday night."

Rick strutted off. Brody turned to Caro, his brow furrowed. "Doesn't Mandy work Saturday night?"

"I'll take care of that. Don't you worry one little bit. Just be there."

"I'm not going."

"You have to, so Rick doesn't concentrate on me. He's got a bit of a crush, but he'll get over it once he realizes I'm taken."

Brody's mouth opened and closed like a fish in a fish tank. "But I—I mean, you and me?"

Caro squeezed his arm. Leaning close she smacked him on the cheek with her lips. "You and me, handsome. Just for show."

He couldn't seem to find any words to respond to her. Not one. But his face turned deep red, redder than Mandy's had earlier.

With a pat to his butt, Caro walked off to join a table of friends. Brody choked on his beer, and Caro laughed.

She couldn't wait for Saturday night.

MADRONA SUNSET (MADRONA ISLAND SERIES 1)

Chapter 10—Friday Night Lights

For as long as Mandy could remember, she loved Friday nights during football season. She'd never been good at sports herself. Her brothers lay claim to the athletic ability in her family. She perfected the art of spectating instead.

Tonight Brody debuted as a coach. She prayed the team did well, not just for him and her brother, but for the entire island. A winning team brought the community together, gave them a sense of pride and purpose.

Caro sat next to Mandy in the packed stands. Her friend nodded briefly but never took her eyes off her nephew. Mandy learned not to bother Caro in sports mom mode. She'd snap your head off and feed it to her young, if she'd had any young. Caro's body moved to and fro, mirroring Connor's movements during the pre-game warm-up. Once the game started, she'd *play* the entire game with him, jerking her body with every tackle, straining her shoulders with every throw, and leaning down during the huddle.

One row above them, Mandy's family had commandeered an entire row of bleachers, coming out in force to support the Sunset Harbor Wildcats, complete with pompons, noisemakers, and blue and gold T-shirts.

Mandy sighed, letting her mind wander back to last night. Caro was up to something, and Mandy didn't trust her one darn bit, especially since she stopped singing Brody's praises and started bragging up Rick. If Brody happened to be around, Caro worked it even harder. Everyone knew Rick adored Caro going back to their high school days. Caro never reciprocated, but a girl had to give Rick points for dogged determination. Maybe Caro hoped to discourage Rick once and for all by pretending to have a thing for Brody.

Something sour and unwelcome settled in the pit of her stomach at the thought of Brody and Caro together, which was stupidly selfish. Unable to see herself with another man who lived for danger, she couldn't have a future with Brody, but maybe Caro could.

A roar went up from the crowd, bringing Mandy back to the here and now. The Tigers kicked off to the Wildcats. Brandon Links ran it back to the Wildcats' forty.

Mandy's gaze sought out Brody standing on the sidelines. He rested his clipboard against one hip. His starting offensive team huddled around him, listening with rapt attention, except for Connor. The quarterback stood a few inches from the huddle, a part of it, but not really a part of it. When her brother stepped into the circle, Connor came alive, pumping his fist, and leaning forward. The quarterback put his hand in the middle of the cluster of teenagers. The boys echoed his "Let's go."

Connor gave Case a thumbs up, but sprinted past Brody as if he didn't exist. Brody's face hardened into an expressionless mask. Her heart went out to him. He didn't deserve Connor's disrespect. She'd talk to Caro about it. Her friend would ground Connor's butt from here to Sunday for his rudeness.

Connor got behind center and barked out the signals. The center hiked the ball. Connor stepped back a few steps and looked for his receivers. He singled out his buddy and the Cats' best receiver, Sid Muldauer. Never taking his eyes off Sid, he didn't even see Brian Stender, wide open and halfway down the field. Connor forced the ball between two defenders. A Tiger defensive back plucked the ball out of the air and streaked down the sidelines to score. Just like that. Easy as pie. The stands on the Sunset Harbor side hushed, as they sat in shocked silence. In the visitor stands across the field, Tiger fans roared their approval. The scoreboard read seven-zero after the extra point was good.

Connor stalked back to the bench. Brody approached him, but the kid turned his back and walked off. Brody's fingers curved into tight fists, and he clenched his jaw.

Mandy turned to Caro who was making short work of her fingernails. "What did you think of Connor on that last play?"

"His receiver wasn't where he was supposed to be." Caro defended her nephew like a mother bear.

"Did you notice he had an open man downfield?" Caro stared at her as if Mandy had just sprouted devil's horns and carried a pitchfork. "No, I didn't see that."

"Brody's been working with him on a method for checking each of his receivers, but Connor's resistant to change." Mandy braced herself for Caro's rebuke.

Caro snorted and flipped her hand, as if dismissing the whole damn thing. "Brody's too technical. Connor plays by instinct."

"Connor might be able to glean some tips from Brody."

"Oh, I don't know. Connor's good enough for high school ball. He'll get the team where they need to go. Brody doesn't need to go screwing with Connor's technique. It's not like scouts are pounding down the doors to recruit him."

"He's only a junior. There's always next year."

"Get real. He's a Native American. How many Native American quarterbacks have you ever seen playing college or pro ball?"

"Sonny Sixkiller for the Washington Huskies."

"Years ago. Besides, his grades aren't good enough." Caro sighed and dismissed Mandy by turning her attention back to the game.

Mandy didn't get it. Caro worked hard to be positive and uplifting. Why didn't she want to encourage her own nephew?

With a heavy sigh, Mandy zipped her mouth shut and decided to avoid that sore subject. Out on the field, the Wildcats offense went three and out then punted. Determination etched on his handsome face, Brody approached Connor on the bench. At the look on Brody's face, Connor's teammates scattered and left him to the wolf. Brody sat down next to him, leaving Mandy a view of only their backs. Connor sat up straight and stared at the field, his spine as stiff and unyielding as his mind.

Brody turned slightly to him, talking and tapping his

clipboard. Finally, Connor turned and looked down at the clipboard, but he kept shaking his head. Brody shook a finger at the kid. Connor jumped to his feet and walked off to join a group of his buddies on the sidelines. Brody's shoulders slumped, and he hunched over his clipboard, making notations.

Mandy wanted the throttle Connor and Caro. If Caro relayed her attitude to Connor, she only served to make matters worse between Brody and him. She just didn't know what she could possibly do about it.

Her heart quickened a little when Brody rose to his feet and stood next to her brother. The two appeared to consult on something. Brody squared his broad shoulders and waved the clipboard around as he drove a point home to Case. Case shook his head and angled his body away from Brody. Her brother cupped his hands to his mouth, shouting at the defense on the field.

Mandy itched to wrap her fingers around her brother's throat or shake some sense into him but it wouldn't help. Brody needed to fight his own battles or completely lose respect of the team and coaches.

What if he threw his hands up at the whole damn business and left? Where would she be?

Of course, she knew the answer to that. She'd be right where she was before he came, obsessing over her dead husband, living in a construction zone, and wallowing in self-pity.

Oh, my God.

Her hand flew to her mouth. She hadn't thought of Frank in over a day. Brody filled her thoughts, her dreams, even her plans for the future. Only he wasn't her future or her past. A small town like this would bore a man like him who craved constant excitement. She'd harbored a hidden fantasy that he might enjoy coaching football so much he'd stay. Forget that thought. Judging by the look on his face, he hated coaching football. Mandy closed her eyes, wishing for a moment of clarity. A collective sigh went up from the people around her. She opened her eyes in time to see another Tiger defender running down the field for a touchdown. Connor had thrown another bad pass on the first play of the series.

Brody threw down his clipboard. Her brother paced the sidelines. Connor avoided them both as he came back to the bench, shoulders slumped, defeat in his posture. This time, Brody made no attempt to talk to the kid. She couldn't blame him. In fact, she wouldn't blame Brody if he walked off this field and never looked back at the football team or the half-finished house.

Or her.

* * * *

Mandy heard Brody's Jeep pull into the driveway. The engine shut off. She was still fully clothed because truth be told, she'd been worried about him and didn't even try to sleep. He'd left right after the game but not gone straight home. Mandy joined her family, friends, and some of the players afterward for pizza. She texted Brody to join them, but he didn't respond. Most likely he'd had enough of the people in this town for a while.

She waited for the sounds of his shoes on the wooden porch or the key in his lock. Nothing.

Mandy crept downstairs to the entryway and opened the front door a crack. In the dim porch light she could make out a figure sitting in the truck. She opened the door and snuck onto the porch, certain he couldn't see her spying on him unless he turned around in his seat.

Brody gripped the steering wheel and stared straight ahead. He must have been sitting like that for several minutes. Then he lowered his head and rested his forehead on the steering wheel in a gesture of utter defeat.

Brody? Defeated? Not possible. Guys like him never gave up, never stopped trying. She longed to comfort him, wrap him in her arms and show him everything would be all right as long as he let people in, instead of shutting them out. Yet she held back. She'd witnessed a private moment. The last thing a man like him wanted was to appear vulnerable.

Undecided, she hesitated, torn between running back in the house and rapping on the Jeep window.

He lifted his head, must have caught sight of her in the rear-view mirror. He jerked his head around. With a wary frown, Brody opened the door and stepped out. Mandy held her breath, not sure what to expect as he mounted the front steps to the porch.

Weariness lined his face. He shifted his gaze downward, almost sheepish. "Hi."

"Hi." Her feet rooted to the spot, as if someone had driven rebar through her feet into the ground.

"It's late." He stated the obvious.

"I know. I wondered where you were."

One corner of his mouth kicked up in a smile that didn't reach his eyes. "Worried about me?"

She opened her mouth to deny any such thing then opted for that gray area between honesty and lying. "I couldn't sleep. I heard a car, but never heard anyone get out."

"I didn't mean to scare you." He limped closer, so close she could smell the mint gum he liked to chew.

"You didn't scare me." Unable to resist, she reached out and touched his arm. His intense blue eyes locked with hers. Her world flipped upside down like an amusement ride gone haywire.

Brody wrapped his strong fingers around her hand on his arm and clutched it to his chest. "Thanks."

"For what?" Her heart pounded so hard, surely he could hear it.

He shrugged. "Just thanks." He glanced up at the stars in sky, as if he expected to find an answer there. Well, she could tell him for a fact those stars didn't give up their secrets.

His fingers tightened around hers. His heart beat steadily

under her palm. Her knees wobbled. Her body swayed. She grabbed a handful of his T-shirt to hold herself upright. Brody grasped her around her waist. Mandy tipped forward until her chest collided with his.

"A little too much wine after the game?" he teased.

"Yeah, drowning my sorrows."

"Drowning sounds like an option."

"I bet you're too good of swimmer for that." She wrapped her arms around his neck. Her body pressed tight against his. He stiffened against her, as if trying to resist.

He sucked in a ragged breath. "Not so much when the current's strong."

"You'll make it. I have faith in you."

His intent gaze peeled away layer after layer of self-protection. She looked away, fearing he saw too much, fearing he'd figure out she'd fallen for him. Placing her hands palms down on his chest, she pushed against him. He didn't resist but released her immediately and stepped back.

Brody ran his hand through his dark hair. "Sorry."

"No need to be sorry. We're—we're just both lonely; combined with the proximity, it's bound to happen."

"Yeah, I suppose." His voice was laced with frustration.

Mandy turned away while she still had enough strength to do so. She stopped with her hand on the doorknob and glanced over her shoulder. He hadn't moved. "Good night."

"Good night."

Mandy shut the door and locked it, even though she couldn't lock out what she really ran from: her feelings for Brody and her fears she'd lose him like she did Frank. Leaning her back against the door, she closed her eyes.

She'd fallen for Brody, for another dangerous man.

"Even desperadoes settle down eventually."

Mandy's eyes popped open. Her heart leapt right into her throat. She could've sworn she'd heard someone speak those words. "Who's here? Case? Guys? This isn't funny."

No one answered her except Sunny who padded into the

living room and stuck his nose in her crotch. She was fucking losing her mind.

She patted Sunny's graying muzzle. "Hey, buddy, did you let a ghost in while I was gone?"

The dog gazed up at her through sightless eyes and sniffed to make sure it was his mom.

"I guess not, huh?"

Sunny turned and ambled back upstairs. It was past his bedtime. And hers.

Still a little spooked, Mandy turned on the TV. She crossed to the couch and shoved the pile of clean laundry to one side. Sitting down, she stared at the screen and tried to figure out what the heck to do about her infatuation with Brody. Just sex she might be able to handle, but the feelings Brody stirred in her ran deeper than sex.

Sometime later she fell asleep, no closer to solving her problem.

Chapter 11—Dancing without the Stars

Brody gathered his courage and limped into the club. Caro waved at him from the back of the room near the small dance floor. Mandy sat next to her. Their gazes clashed for a brief moment before Mandy looked away. She looked hot in a simple, fuzzy pink sweater with her hair curled around her face. He liked her dressed up or dressed down. Fuck, he just flat out liked everything about her.

Between Mandy and Caro sat a very pleased Rick. Of course the fucker was pleased. Two hot women flanked him. He'd probably never enjoyed such action in his life.

Rick smiled at Brody, totally guileless, a truly nice guy, which made Brody feel like shit for wanting to slam his fist into Rick's face just because he could. This entire thing had been Brody's stupid idea, and he'd regretted it the second Caro put their plan into action.

Brody sank into the only empty chair at the square table, avoiding the curious stares of the women in the room and the accusing glares of the men. He'd heard the talk around town. They blamed him for the team losing last night.

What the fuck?

He rubbed his throbbing forehead and glanced at Mandy. Did she blame him, too? He needed to get Connor under control. How could one teenage boy cause a big, bad Green Beret this much grief?

He'd wanted so badly to walk off that field and forget he'd ever heard of this town. But then he'd be a quitter, and that wouldn't fucking do at all. He might be fighting the entire team and the other coaches, but he could help the team if they'd only listen. Perhaps, last night's loss would drive that point home. Somehow, he doubted it. Connor's pigheadedness went deeper than that.

He rubbed the aching muscles of his bad leg. That damn thing had cramped up like a son-of-a-bitch during the game, probably because he'd done too much pacing and stamping on the sidelines. He honestly couldn't remember a more frustrating time in his entire life. The Wildcats weren't his only problem.

There was Mandy.

Oh, hell, yeah. She popped in his head at the worst of times with promises for the best of times, at least in his stupid-assed dreams.

Last night, he'd bit the side of his cheek until he tasted blood to keep himself from blurting out an invitation to his bed. God knows how that would have ended up.

Sally, the fill-in bartender, dropped a beer in front of him.

"I didn't order this."

"Rick did."

Brody turned to Rick, feeling like an even bigger shit. "Oh, hey, thanks."

"You're welcome, buddy." Rick grinned at him, having a helluva lot better time than Brody and judging by Mandy's stiff posture, better than Mandy.

Brody dodged Caro's dramatic gestures as she almost smacked him in the face. She didn't even notice as she kept up her running dialogue. White noise. He didn't hear a word she said. Instead, he tried his damnedest to keep his eyes off Mandy, let Rick move in, let something between them grow. That'd be so much better for her. Brody didn't have a thing to offer but a whole lot of baggage, the worst of which he'd kept from her. He shuddered to think how much she'd hate him when she found out the real story.

Caro linked her arm with Brody's, like they were a real couple. He managed a feeble smile but knew it never reached his eyes.

His stomach churned at the thought of Mandy and Rick together, but he'd be a good soldier and do his part for the cause. Damn, he hated his sense of duty, sometimes. Then he remembered a hot desert night sitting in the darkness with nothing to do but wait. Those conversations came flooding back. Frank talked about his wife with reverence, like she was a saint.

She needs a good man, not an adrenaline junkie like us. Guys who feed off danger are so not what she needs.

Yeah, Brody was so not what she needed.

Ever. *So don't get any ideas, dumbshit.*

Hell, he already had ideas, too many of them.

He caught Caro's eye. She raised a black eyebrow and flicked her gaze in Rick's direction. Brody nodded subtly. Time for their plan to be put into play despite the churning in his stomach.

"Rick, you're a big baseball fan, right?" Caro slid closer to Brody. Brody angled his body away from her. She kicked him under the table with the toe of her cowboy boot.

Damn, that hurt and right on his bad leg.

Mandy watched the two of them, biting that plump lower lip. She'd worn this conservative shade of pink lipstick tonight that did it for him more than any cherry red lipstick ever did. His dick liked it, too. Unfortunately. He shifted in his chair, unable to get comfortable.

"Yeah, I, uh, love baseball. What do you think of baseball, Caro?" Rick blinked rapidly and rubbed his cheek.

"I hate baseball." Caro's pinched face reminded Brody of a dried up apple. If it wasn't that he was supposed to be her partner in crime, he'd be laughing his ass off.

Mandy's brow wrinkled as she regarded the two conspirators with suspicion. "Caro, you're a bigger baseball fan than I am."

"Not anymore." Caro seemed to be drowning, and Brody didn't do anything to rescue her. "Rick, they're playing Mandy's favorite song. Why don't you ask her to dance?"

Rick, who'd been staring at Caro like a lovelorn rooster, sat up straight and frowned. "Uh, yeah, sure." He turned to Mandy with a reluctant smile. "Uh, Mandy, do you wanna dance?"

Mandy glared at Caro, while Brody pasted his best innocent look on his face and played dumb. Really dumb. Rick stood and held out his hand to Mandy. Backed into a corner, Mandy followed Rick to the dance floor.

"You're no help." Caro poked Brody in the arm.

Brody rubbed his arm. "Hey, quit beating up on me."

"You're screwing this up. Do you want her to find the right guy or not?"

"You had it handled. What did you want me to do?" Brody couldn't keep the defensiveness out of his voice. He also kept one eye trained on Rick and Mandy.

"He's drooling all over me. We need to get his attention off me and onto Mandy." Caro jabbed her thumb in the direction of the dance floor. "He's looking over her shoulder right now at me."

Yeah, well, Rick had to look someplace. "Don't you think he's holding her a little too close?" Brody spoke through clenched teeth.

Caro narrowed her eyes and studied him more closely. "What are you talking about? You could drive a tank between them. Their chemistry wouldn't light a nightlight." When Brody didn't respond, Caro snapped her fingers in front of his face.

Brody forced his gaze back to Caro. His chest burned like he'd eaten too many jalapeños. "Maybe he's the wrong guy. Do you have a Tums?"

"No, I don't fucking have a Tums. Get with the program. This was your idea."

Brody opened and closed his mouth, scratched his head, battled with his emotions. It had been his idea. She was right. He needed to play along, do a better job, even if his heart wasn't in it. This charade was for Mandy's own good. "I'll try harder."

"Don't sound so glum about it. Dance with me and make it look convincing." Caro stood up and headed for the dance floor before he could respond.

Brody limped after her. She stood on the dance floor, tapping her foot impatiently, and opened her arms. Brody put his arms loosely around her waist. Caro yanked him against her.

Brody splayed his hands on her waist and pushed her back to a respectable distance. "I suppose you're going to insist on leading, too?" he grumbled.

"You're damn right. Now hold me like I'm your lover, not your sister."

"Not gonna happen. This is as good as it gets. If you don't like it, find some other guy to be your pretend boyfriend."

Caro blew out an exasperated sigh. "One more time. Whose idea was this?"

Brody looked away, feeling a little sheepish. "Mine."

His annoyed partner rolled her eyes and yanked him closer to Mandy and Rick.

"You're leading again." Brody took control and spun her around. She stomped on his foot with her boot heel. Brody yelped, drawing the stares of several other dancers, including Rick and Mandy.

Pissed, Brody dipped Caro low and stared straight into her eyes with his best interrogation glare. She stuck her tongue out at him, righted herself, and went back to leading.

With a sigh, Brody gave in, knowing several sets of prying eyes watched them. Looking over his shoulder, he saw Mandy laugh at something Rick said. Brody scowled. He'd never heard Rick say anything even remotely funny so what the fuck was up with that? Rick grinned at her, as if really seeing her for the first time. The two of them were almost eye to eye because of similar heights. She'd be taller than him if she wore heels, which gave Brody a twinge of satisfaction.

"You're hopeless. They're never going to buy you and me together." Caro nuzzled his neck, and he stiffened.

"So we tell them we're having a lover's quarrel." Thank God the song ended just then. Brody released Caro and backed away from her. She shook her head, grabbed his hand, and dragged him back to the table.

Rick and Mandy stood on the dance floor, still talking and

holding hands, which only stoked Brody's increasingly foul mood. Caro studied him with interest, and he knew damn well she wouldn't be able to keep her mouth shut.

She wasn't.

"They're getting along quite well, despite a rocky start." Caro gave him a Mona Lisa smile as Rick and Mandy stayed on the dance floor for another dance.

"Yeah, great." Brody leaned back in his chair and crossed his arms over his chest. They weren't supposed to hit it off this well, this quickly. It was supposed to be more difficult than this.

"It's hard for a person to step out of their comfort zone, especially when that involves risks."

"Mandy needs to take chances." Brody didn't like the pointed way Caro looked at him—not one damn bit—as if he was missing something.

"Most of us do, don't you think? Life's pretty dull without risks."

"Sure." Brody took chances every day in his chosen career. He lived to take chances.

"Sometimes emotional risks are even harder to take than physical ones."

Brody chewed on that one for a moment. Eyes hooded, he squinted at Caro. "I suppose."

"They're such a cute couple, aren't they?"

"Fucking wonderful."

"I'm glad you came up with this idea, Brody. So unselfish of you."

Oh, hell, yeah, that was him, king of the gracious and selfless. Only he didn't feel either right now. And here came the happy couple back to grace them with their presence.

Rick grinned like a chimpanzee with a bushel of bananas. "We thought we'd leave you guys alone for a moment to work out your problems."

"We worked them out, all right. We broke up." Brody couldn't staunch the flow of words from his mouth. He moved just in time to avoid another well-placed kick from Caro.

"He's kidding."

"No, really, I'm not. We're better as friends. I'm not Caro's type." Brody patted Caro's hand, faking his concern. "No harm, no foul. Right, honey?"

Caro looked ready to shove one of her boots down his throat.

Standing, Brody nodded to the ladies and shook Rick's hand. "Sorry, but I need to see Harvey about some business. Have a good evening."

Brody hobbled hard and fast away from the table, unable to take it any longer. This dumb-ass idea of his had backfired on him. He hated seeing Mandy with another man, even if it was the best thing for the both of them.

Mandy and Rick weren't supposed to get along so well. Was Brody that easy to replace?

He hated himself for being jealous. He never got jealous.

Now what was he going to do about it?

* * * *

Sunday night Mandy walked into the empty bar at closing time. Caro glanced up as she pulled wineglasses out of the commercial dishwasher and slid them into the wineglass rack over the counter.

"I was hoping I'd find you still here," Mandy said, stalking her friend like a she-lion stalking an antelope.

Caro smiled innocently at her. "What gives?"

Mandy frowned at her friend, more than a little annoyed at Caro and Brody's weird performance last night at the dance. They'd literally shoved her and Rick together then faked this relationship with each other more transparent than a clean window.

"What the hell was all that about last night?" She slid onto a barstool and leaned her elbows on the counter.

"What?" Caro's big brown eyes widened in mock

innocence.

"Don't play stupid. Brody and you? Together? Never happen. So what's really going on?"

"You and Rick seemed cozy enough." Caro skirted her question in a typical Caro manner.

"We aren't. Not at all. He's a nice guy, but that's it." Mandy bristled more than she meant to, giving into the annoyance.

"But you're interested in someone else."

"No, I am not." Mandy sat up straight in her chair and fixed Caro with a deadly glare.

"You're moving on, Mandy. Like it or not. You're interested in another man. A man very much alive and very much interested in you." Caro laughed and leaned against the back counter. "Brody was jealous as hell; it was a sight to see."

"He was not."

"Sure was. He looked ready to drown Rick in the toilet and throw you over his shoulder and take you to bed."

Erotic images of a naked Mandy draped over Brody's bare shoulder as he carried her to his room dominated her thoughts. He'd swat her ass a few times and toss her on the bed before he—

"That good, huh? Has it already happened or just in your dreams?"

"No, it hasn't happened, and it won't." Mandy's face burned, and she ducked her head, fearing Caro would further read her mind.

"Why the fuck not? Fuck the guy. I mean screw his brains out. Do it all night until neither one of you can stand on your own two feet. That's what you need, honey." Caro poured a glass of water and handed it to Mandy. "Getting a lot hot in here for you, isn't it?"

Mandy scrubbed her face with her hands and sighed, abandoning her denial. "I can't stop thinking about him, his smile, his hot blue eyes, his bare chest, the way he watches me like I'm his next meal. Everything. But I—"

Caro held up a hand and stopped her in mid-sentence. "Don't say it. Don't even say it. Frank is gone. G. O. N. E. Gone, never to return. Brody works the same type of job as Frank. Get the fuck over it and move on. Jobs can be changed with the right motivation. Brody wants you, you want him. Now that's motivation. Make it happen and quit being a whiny bitch."

Mandy's mouth fell open, and she stared at Caro, unable to believe her harsh words. Finally, she had to laugh. "Tough love or what?"

"Yeah, tough love. Time to put on the big girl panties, quit wallowing in self-pity and fear, and get on with your life guilt free and ready to take advantage of all life has to offer."

"I want to, I really do. I just don't know if I can take another risk with a man like that."

"You can, and you will because if you don't, I'm going to kick your ass all the way to the mainland." Caro leaned in close to her, fingers splayed on the counter, her dark eyes blazing.

"I'll try."

"Don't try. Do. Get it? Do."

Mandy nodded and swallowed, unable to respond around the lump clogging her throat.

Chapter 12—Choices

On Wednesday Brody pounded one last finish nail and stood back and admired his handiwork. Gone were the sawhorse countertops. The kitchen looked like a kitchen. The custom cherry cabinets, once stacked in a corner, gleamed in the afternoon sun pouring in the window. He ran a hand over the wood's smooth surface, admiring the quality. He opened a drawer, liking how with a soft nudge, it slowly closed with a neat click. The large window over the sink looked out over glistening water in the cove.

At least, he felt good about one thing in his life. Hell, he'd even like to cook in this kitchen. Once the countertop guys installed the granite and he hung the upper cabinets, it'd be good to go. He glanced at his watch. Case should be here anytime to help. He didn't look forward to seeing the guy more than the once a day at practice, but he couldn't hold up the heavy cabinets and attach them to studs at the same time. He'd rather have found someone else to help, but Case had a teacher's day off today.

The front door opened. Case walked in carrying a tool chest and dressed for the job in ratty jeans and a torn T-shirt. He sat a carrier containing two cups of coffee on top of a stack of papers littering the dining room table.

"Hey, thanks." Brody tried for the friendly approach, not that it'd worked before on the guy. He reached for a coffee and took a long, appreciative sip of the strong, black brew. Just the way he liked it. "Good stuff."

"Yeah." Case dug through his tool chest and pulled out his tool belt. Obviously, the guy didn't plan on making much conversation.

Brody explained what needed to be done next. Case nodded without comment. Like a well-oiled machine, they went to work, not wasting a spare minute on chit-chat. In a few hours they'd hung the upper cabinets and added the trim.

"Looks good." Case ran a hand over the cherry wood on

the doors.

"I think Mandy will be pleased."

Case chewed on his lower lip, cleaned the crap off a barstool, and sat down. "This is a much better job than Frank would've ever done. He wasn't much for detail work. Get it done and get on with something else."

Brody had to smile. Yup, that was Frank. "Not a perfectionist, huh?"

"Nope." Case hung his hands between his knees and stared out the window.

A realization slammed into Brody. Case missed Frank, too. After all, they'd been childhood buddies. "Frank was a hellavua guy from what I hear."

"Yeah. Never be another like him."

Brody nodded. Case didn't know the half of it, and as far as Brody was concerned he never would.

Their easy conversation about Frank surprised Brody. Maybe he'd reached a truce of sorts with Case. A truce Brody figured he'd shatter with his next words. "I'm thinking of benching Connor tomorrow night."

Instead of expressing shock or anger, Case rubbed his chin, still staring out the window. "He's been pushing your buttons."

"Yeah, he's outwardly defiant, challenging my role with the team."

"The offense is in your hands. You know best. Do what you need to do, just know we'll all suffer the consequences or reap the rewards."

"It's not just about winning. The kid's talented. If he'd just listen and improve his play, I think he might be able to get a scholarship."

"From this little town? No one will pay attention to him." Case shook his head, as if he, too, bought into that line of logic.

"They will if we win State," Brody pointed out.

"You really believe that?"

"I know it, but he needs to improve his technique."

"Good luck with that. The kid's as pigheaded as his Aunt Caro." Regret flickered in Case's eyes, and Brody did a double-take. He'd bet his Purple Heart there was history between Case and Caro. *Interesting.* He filed that tidbit away for future reference.

"So you'll support me if I bench him? Just for the first half of the game to prove my point."

Case frowned and walked to the open French doors, staring out at the water. He clasped his hands behind his back, his body tense. Finally he turned back around. "Yeah, I will, but it could backfire. He could walk off the team, or we could lose another game. The locals will crucify us both if that happens."

Brody nodded. He'd never considered Case's side in all this. As a new head coach, Case had something to prove. Being saddled with Brody, a rookie at coaching, didn't help his cause any. But Brody knew football. Come hell or high water he'd find a way to impart his knowledge to his offense, even if he had to force feed it to their stubborn teenage brains.

They shared a beer on the back porch in the shade of hundred-year-old madronas, talking football and fishing, two things they had in common. Brody couldn't say they'd become friends, but they'd definitely reached a point of civility.

"Good to see my sister dating again." Case spoke casually, but the way he eyed Brody was anything but casual, as if gauging his reaction.

Brody sure as hell didn't plan on showing any weakness. He swallowed and forced his expression into an indifferent mask. "Rick's a great guy." Damn, but it killed him to say that, even if it was the truth. The guy *was* drop-dead dull. Brody took a little solace in that.

"Rick's just want she needs. Stable, dependable, good family."

As in Brody was just what she didn't need. Yeah, Brody got it. Just last night, he'd gone to the VC and noticed them sitting across the street in the small café having dinner. He'd slinked into the club, downed one drink, and gotten the hell out of there, not wanting to be around if they came in after dinner. His gut churned at the thought of Rick kissing Mandy, holding her close, sleeping in her bed.

Case eyed him with suspicion, leaving Brody to wonder if his expression gave him away. "Everyone in town is glad to see her with Rick."

Well, whoop-dee-do. Mandy and Rick only had that one date to his knowledge, yet it sounded like the whole damn town was planning a wedding. "I'm sure they are."

"Yeah, my family's thrilled. We'd hate to see her get her heart broken again or end up with another guy in a dangerous career. You know, like a cop or fireman."

Or a slightly damaged soldier for hire. Brody turned away from Case and started cleaning up their construction mess.

Case gathered his tools, put away his tool belt, and headed for the door. "See ya at three."

"Yeah. Three." Brody couldn't fucking wait.

He'd give Connor until game night. If the kid didn't shape up, he'd follow through, which would either prove his point or alienate the entire team and town. On top of that, his actions might pound one more nail in the coffin of Case's head coaching career.

Brody wanted that state championship as badly as anyone, but the team had a long way to go before that happened. Just like he still had a long way to go to get over Frank's death and his part in it. And even further to go to wipe Mandy out of his system because somehow she'd gotten into a place he kept locked up tight.

Damned if he knew how to boot her cute ass out that door.

Chapter 13—Power Tools

She wasn't sure what had gotten into her, but Mandy spent her rare day off on Thursday cleaning house. She recycled the newspapers and magazines and folded the clean laundry and put it in its proper place. After which she dusted and polished the woodwork, swept the unfinished floors, and cleaned the bathrooms.

Rick called and invited her to a movie, but she declined. As much as she tried to force herself to like him, his annoying habits turned her off. For example, the man grunted for no reason at all, like a nervous tic. He flossed at the dinner table after a meal. When she talked, he rarely looked her in the eyes. Instead, his gaze darted everywhere else.

For the past couple days, she'd turned down every invitation, yet he showed no signs of giving up. In fact, if anything, her disinterest egged him on to the point where she suspected he might actually have transferred his crush from Caro to her.

Poor guy.

She really needed to get her feet wet with dating, even if it was with someone like him. At least, her heart would be safe. She'd never truly be able to give her heart away to an emotionally unsafe guy. So why not develop a comfortable relationship with a safe guy?

Because she didn't want him.

Mandy leaned her head against the cool window glass and closed her eyes, but she couldn't shut out the one guy who kept popping into her brain, and that one guy wasn't Frank. Not anymore.

On cue Brody walked in her door. They'd barely seen each other in the past few days. She fought to keep a welcoming smile from crossing her lips, but she lost the battle.

He smiled back, a genuine happy-to-see-you smile. "I'm surprised you're home." He stopped dead just inside the door and did a shocked double-take. "What the hell happened to the house?"

"It's my day off. I thought I'd clean it up a little. The kitchen looks so good, I had to do something to the rest of the place."

"There's furniture in here that hasn't seen the light of day in years. You've unburied stuff I didn't know existed."

"If it's too much for you, I could mess it back up given a few hours."

He waved his hands and shook his head. "No. No. Let's go with this. It'll be a unique adventure in tidiness. I'm ready if you are."

She was ready all right. Too ready. Too willing. And too able. "Have you eaten? I was about to throw a chicken breast on the barbecue."

He hesitated, glancing toward the door, as if seeking an escape route. Turning to face her, he nodded. "Yeah, I'd like one. Want me to do the honors?"

"I'll make a salad and cook up some potatoes."

"Sounds great." He took the tray of chicken breasts and carried them outside.

Mandy stared after him. The situation struck her as too familiar, too right and yet so wrong. They sounded like an old married couple. She forced her feet to move and busied herself in her gorgeous kitchen with the new granite countertops.

A few minutes later, she joined Brody on the deck he'd completed last week. A plastic lawn chair beckoned to her tired body. She sat down and looked out at the water. Summer was giving way to fall. Most of the boats in the channel had disappeared, leaving only the sounds of water lapping at the shore and the honking of the Canadian geese in the sky.

Brody leaned against the deck railing, his body loose and relaxed for once. One hand dangled off the side of the rail, the other he'd tucked in his jeans. A little hint of stubble grew along his strong jawline, contrasting with those pale blue eyes. The strong, chiseled features of his face softened as he turned to look at her. The tender look in his eyes warmed her very soul. Her heart fluttered like a one-winged butterfly trying to gain purchase in the breeze. She longed to rake her fingernails over the rough stubble and bury her fingers in his dark hair.

"Brody, I don't know how to ever thank you for all the work you've done around here."

He shrugged, seeming almost embarrassed. The man didn't accept compliments well. "Thanks, I needed to do it as much as you needed it done."

"Well, you've gone above and beyond."

"I like to keep busy, and I enjoy this kind of work." His mouth, usually so tight and uncompromising, parted slightly. He seemed at ease, even at home. Like he belonged here.

Belonged here? Another man who craved danger and adventure?

Who was she kidding?

Her stomach nose-dived into a swimming pool without water, hitting bottom with a hard slam. Mandy hugged herself tight. He'd finish this *mission* and move on because that's what guys like him did. Sure, Frank put down roots, but he didn't return to them often. She'd spent many more nights without him than with him during their marriage. She didn't want that again, even if by some miracle Brody wanted more than a friendship.

"Are you okay?" Brody stood next to her, his eyes full of concern and that concern was her undoing. Grasping her hands, he pulled her to her feet and wrapped her in his arms.

Instead of pushing out of his arms, she allowed herself the luxury of being comforted by a strong man. She was tired, so tired, of being strong, of fighting this battle alone, never certain if she was winning or losing. The pressures of turning the B&B into a viable business, working full-time, and starting to live her life again weighed her down, smothering her, threatening to crush her.

He felt so good, so solid, so gentle yet tough, a man a woman could depend on when the storms raged outside her door.

Every carefully controlled emotion busted lose, like water surging out of a broken water main with no shutoff valve. The tears filled her eyes, rolled down her cheeks, and soaked Brody's shirt, as he held her in his strong arms. She didn't have to be the strong one anymore, he could be that guy for her, at least for a little while. She ignored every warning bell blaring in her head and clung to him.

Sobs wracked every cell in her body. She cried like she hadn't cried since the week after Frank died. She cried for all the things she lost that day. She cried for the end of her life as she'd planned it. And she cried for the new future she wanted but knew she couldn't allow.

Brody held her through it all, whispered words of comfort in her ear, gentle, sweet words. He called her pet names, names she'd never expected to hear from another man, but she heard them from him. They didn't sound strange. They sounded right, so very right. His hot breath tickled her ear and sent shivers through her entire body.

And she loved hearing the words as much as she loved being in his arms. Guys like Rick didn't stand a chance when it came to Brody's magnetic pull.

She should push Brody away.

Now. Right now.

Hello? Arms, get rid of this guy.

Not happening, but a lot of other things were happening, such as her noticing how good his hard body felt against hers, how surprisingly soft his hair was, and how much she loved the scratch of his stubble against her tear-stained cheeks.

Mandy wrapped her arms around his neck, blinked a few times, and gazed up at him through blurry eyes. He looked down at her, his expression unguarded and tender, sweet, kind. Things a person would never see at first glance because he hid that side so well.

He dabbed at her tears with the pad of one rough thumb. "You okay?" Concern softened his blue eyes.

She nodded, unable to trust her voice. He didn't release

her, just continued to stare at her with his hand cradling her chin. He bent down and kissed her cheek, cupped her face in his hands, and smiled his sexy, crooked smile.

Her body fell at his feet and worshipped the porch he stood on. Mandy shoved all her misgivings and guilt into a mental safe, slammed the door shut, and locked it. But safes could be opened another day, another time, allowing all the baggage to tumble out. But for now, she tucked the key away for safekeeping.

Parting her lips, Mandy waited, praying Brody compartmentalized his reservations in his own credit union vault.

They'd both worry about the repercussions in the morning.

"Mandy, I—" His blue gaze searched her face. She read the indecision in his eyes, along with the stark need. "This isn't a good idea."

"I think it is." She leaned into him. Her hips pressed against his mid-section. His erection pressed against her, proof he wasn't immune to her body, any more than she was to his.

"Are you sure you know what you're doing?"

"Positive."

"What about—uh, Rick?" He didn't say *Frank*, yet it hung in the hot, heavy air between them.

"Rick's just a friend." And Frank, well, Frank wasn't here. She'd pay tomorrow, but tonight she needed a man. *This man.*

"This is so wrong in so many ways." Despite his arguments, his body didn't seem to be arguing. In fact, he wrapped his arms around her waist and pulled her closer.

"Then why does it feel so right? I'm tired of fighting this thing between us."

"Oh, hell, so am I." Brody angled his head, and she knew he was going to kiss her. The first touch of his lips on hers ignited a spark of passion deep inside her. She needed this strong man tonight, and she wouldn't stop until she got him.

He captured her lower lip between his teeth and sucked, ever so gently. Mandy groaned and buried her fingers in his hair. His hands moved up her back and molded her body to his. He released her lower lip and pressed both lips against hers. She opened to him, and his tongue slipped inside, exploring, tasting, tantalizing. She kissed him back with all the passion she'd locked inside her body for the past three years, maybe longer.

Brody backed her against the railing, picking her up so her butt rested on the rail. Parting her legs, he moved between them. Not even for a beat did his mouth release hers, which took talent.

He devoured her with his mouth, like a famished man who'd been on a training mission for hours and had just come back to the mess hall. She wrapped her legs around his thighs and gave it right back to him.

Mandy inhaled the fresh scent of him, a combination of soap and the great outdoors; nothing about this man would ever be confined to an apartment in the city. He needed space, just as he needed adventure. The only adventure he'd get on this island revolved around the latest drama at the club, the football team, and perhaps in bed. She doubted it'd be enough. But for tonight, it would do.

He drew back, beads of sweat on his forehead. Even though the outside temperature was mild, obviously his inside temperature burned as hot as hers. His heavy-lidded eyes focused on her well-kissed lips, slightly swollen from his earlier assault.

"God, Mandy. I want you," he croaked.

"I want you, Brody, so bad I can hardly stand it." She clutched his upper arms, holding tight, fearing any moment he might change his mind and leave her cold and alone.

"I don't want either of us to have regrets." His blue eyes searched hers, looking for answers.

"That's for tomorrow. We have tonight."

His mouth crooked in his so-familiar, sexy half-grin.

"Isn't that a song?"

"Probably."

"What about dinner?" He glanced at the barbecue.

"It can wait." She tossed back her hair and gave him her best come-hither look. He grinned broadly, showing an expanse of straight, white teeth.

"I like the way you think." He lifted her off the railing and placed her firmly on the porch. "You're sure?"

"I'm positive."

"What about Fr—"

She held a finger to his lips. "No, not tonight. Tonight is about us. No one else. Got it?"

He nodded, a grave expression on his face, as if he didn't quite believe her. She'd show him. Somehow. Brody grabbed her hand and headed for the house. He flicked off the gas barbecue on the way be. Mandy put the chicken in the refrigerator and locked the doors and turned off the lights in case any nosy relatives dropped by uninvited.

Picking her up, he carried her upstairs to her room as if she weighed nothing. He laid her on the bed and gazed down at her for a moment.

She held her arms out to him. "Come here."

He did. Lord, how she loved an obedient man, at least, when it came to some things. He rolled onto his back, taking her with him so she lay on top of his long, muscled frame. His lips found hers again. He kissed her thoroughly, his lips roaming down her jaw, to her earlobe and neck until he rained little kisses on her collarbone. She moaned when he nipped at the sensitive skin.

Brody flipped her onto her back on the bed. Raising up, he studied her for a moment. Supporting himself with one hand, he pulled his shirt off and tossed it on the floor. Mandy slid her hands across his bare chest. She loved how his coarse chest hairs felt against her fingertips. She flicked her tongue across one nipple, and his eyes rolled back in his head. He bared his teeth as if holding back took everything he had.

Mandy didn't want him to hold back. She had a few tricks up her sleeve. She trailed kisses to his other nipple, licked it, and sucked.

"Oh, fuck." He arched his back, pressing his hips into hers. Rolling off her, he pulled her into a sitting position. "Your turn, honey. Let me see you."

Mandy hesitated. She was fat. Surely, he was used to skinny women or women in incredible shape, not some out-of-shape, frumpy, thirty-something woman like her.

"Are you having second thoughts?"

"No, no, nothing like that." Mandy leaned forward and kissed his mouth. "I don't want you to see me."

He frowned, confusion written across his rugged features. "I don't understand."

"I'm fat." There she'd said it. The obvious. He would hate her body. He'd be repulsed by it.

Instead, he chuckled and kissed her right back. "You're not fat. I think your body is curvy and sexy. I like a woman with a little meat on her bones. You're just fine the way you are, and I really want to see you."

"Are you sure?" Doubt battled with lust. And was it a battle, but lust was stronger. "Okay." With shaking fingers, she unbuttoned her blouse and slid it off her shoulders. It joined his T-shirt on the floor. His eyes lit up with desire, banishing all doubts from her mind that he might find her body unattractive.

"Allow me." He reach behind her and unclasped her bra with the ease of an experienced man. Pulling it off, he stared at her breasts, which she'd always considered too large. Only the way he looked at her, he obviously didn't agree.

"You are one hot woman." Gently pushing her back to the bed, Brody lay beside her and kissed the flesh near her nipple. He cupped her other breast and squeezed it.

"You're one hot man."

"Then we're even."

"I'm a hot man?"

"Honey, if you're a man, I'm a woman. Either way, it works out."

He went back to his task, which appeared to be melting every doubt which still lingered into a pile of molten lust. That secret area between her legs tingled with anticipation. Her nipples pebbled under his adept ministrations until she swore she might come just from his mouth. She'd never done that before, but hey, a first time for everything.

As if sensing she teetered on the edge, Brody rolled off her. He pulled his jeans down, followed by his boxers to reveal—my, oh, my—a very large cock. She pushed comparisons from her mind because she'd only been with one other man to compare. She couldn't fall into that trap because one man was dead and one was—she swallowed—very alive. And well. And happy to see her.

"Do you like my, uh, tool?"

She nodded, unable to speak. Brody stood there and didn't move. The longer she stared, the more uncertainty deepened his features. Surely, they'd gotten beyond that. She followed his eyes downward, past his impressive, um, tool, and gasped.

"Oh, Brody." She reached out a hand to touch the massive scars and burns on the lower half of his body. She'd never realized the extent of the damage because it'd all been concealed below the belt. She traced one particularly nasty scar as it zigged and zagged from a few inches below his privates past his knees. Tracing back upward, she stopped short of his balls. He shuddered, his body tense and rigid.

"Do I repulse you?"

"Repulse me? Of course not. But does it hurt?" She met his gaze, seeing the fear reflected in his blue eyes. He honestly thought she'd be turned off by his nasty scars? Obviously other women had been.

"Not much. Not anymore."

"At least it didn't affect your—um—"

"Tool?"

"Uh, yeah, your very large power tool."

He smiled, the tension dropping off his face. "Your turn, honey. Let's see the rest of the goods, 'cause I love what I'm seeing so far."

Fine, she'd let him see her overly pudgy hips and fat tummy. See if he still wanted to sleep with her. Maybe his *tool* would shrivel at the sight of her. She glanced up at him as she shimmied out of her jeans.

Not a chance in hell. He almost drooled, like a wolf prowling after a very tasty morsel and ready to pounce. Her somewhat conservative panties came next.

"You're beautiful."

"Promise?"

"Never tease a horny man." In one swift movement, she found herself sprawled on his lap. Her stomach pressed against his erection and her ass was up in the air. He rubbed her bare butt, teasing her with each stroke. The moistness between her legs increased, while her head spun with dizzying speed.

He smacked her ass with a solid smack. Not once. Not twice. But three times. It stung but not as much as it turned her on.

Damn.

Two could play this game. She rubbed her stomach against his erection in a circular motion, while pressing against him. He rewarded her work with a tortured groan.

"I really need you inside me. We can take it slower later." Later? She'd just committed herself to a later. What the heck? Why not? A girl only lived once. Tonight she'd celebrate taking risks; tomorrow she could go back to her boring, staid, sexless life.

"I thought you'd never ask." Brody lifted her off his lap and fished a condom out of his wallet, tore it open with his teeth, and rolled it onto his cock. His efficiency impressed her.

"You just happened to have one in your wallet?"

He ducked his head, almost embarrassed. "Yeah, I always carry one. It's part of my military training to be prepared."

"I thought that was the Boy Scouts."

"Honey, I'm no Boy Scout."

"I'm glad for that."

He pulled Mandy onto his lap so she faced him and her legs straddled his body. She grabbed his broad shoulders for balance, feeling his muscles flex under her fingers. His erection pressed hard and heavy against her crotch.

"Are you wet for me, Mandy?"

She nodded. Oh, boy was she ready, primed like a pump and craving some satisfaction. It'd been too, too long. "You're going to take me like this?"

"You got a problem with that?" His crooked grin warmed her heart and something else.

"What about your leg?"

"Leg? What leg?" He kept grinning, as if the pain were nothing compared to having her, as if she were the most desirable woman ever.

"Did I say something about a leg? Get to work, mister." Frank had been her only lover. Which was about to change, and strangely enough, she felt no regrets. At least not tonight.

Brody held her waist and lowered her onto his big boy who'd reported for duty and stood at attention. As the head of his cock split her opening, she leaned forward and kissed Brody, a wet, sloppy we're-gonna-have-a-great-time kiss. Brody kissed her back, sucking her tongue into his mouth and moving his lips over hers with a demanding hunger. Inch by glorious inch, he filled her with his cock and his strong presence.

"Damn, you're so incredibly tight. You can't imagine how good my dick feels inside you. I don't want to hurt you, but it's so hard not to just take you with one stroke." Brody spoke through gritted teeth. Sweat poured off his forehead, and his arms shook.

Mandy wriggled her body, angling her hips downward to take more of him, letting him know she could handle him. He lowered her down the last few inches until their bodies pressed tightly together. He filled her up inside like nothing she'd ever imagined. Her body pulsed around him, glorying in the feeling of him buried so deep.

He lifted her up part way and lowered her back down again and again, maintaining a slow, torturous rhythm. She thought she'd die. He appeared to feel the same way. The veins stood out on his neck. His breathing was labored. She leaned back, driving him even deeper.

She felt his cock twitch and knew he'd come soon. A few more thrusts, and Brody came with a thunderous roar. Witnessing the mind-blowing joy on his face caused her to follow right after.

He pulled her down on top of him and held her tight, as she lay against him, eyes closed, muddled brain attempting to process what just happened.

But tonight wasn't about thinking. Mandy switched her brain off and allowed herself to just feel the strong man underneath her.

She enjoyed the moment.

The regrets could come later. Much later.

Right now she'd live in the moment.

* * * *

Brody woke to a warm woman cuddled against him. He slipped his arm around her and snuggled down under the covers. Damn, but she felt good, all soft and pliable against him. She'd been a tigress in bed, blindsiding him with her passion and willingness to give as good as she got. They'd fucked late into the night until his limbs turned limp and his body collapsed. Sated, drained, and satisfied, he'd fallen asleep with her in his arms. It appeared he woke the same way.

He was hard for her. Again.

Fuck.

He couldn't recall another woman who drove him as crazy as this one. He wanted her. Again. Every day. Every night. And in every which way. On top. Underneath. Doggie style on the counter. On the porch. Under the stars. Tied up. Untied. You name it, he wanted to do it that way with her.

He'd always been a missionary style guy himself. Get in, get it done, and get the hell out before the woman expected more than a quick screw. But with Mandy, he'd lingered, enjoying the journey as much as the actual act. He'd loved making her writhe underneath him, making her beg for him, cry out his name in the heat of passion, and come for him while he held her tight in his arms.

She'd taken him places he'd never been. Even when he swore he'd seen it all, done it all, but she showed him how little he knew about women. And especially about her.

He wanted to know more, a lot more, and he wanted to take God's sweet time educating himself.

He stilled and closed his eyes, savoring the moment, knowing it could all end any second. Mandy stirred beside him. He squinted at her.

"Brody, we can't do this."

"I know." Boy, did he ever know because even now he wasn't sure he'd recover, but tell that to his dick. The boy had game.

"No regrets?" She rolled onto her stomach and rested her chest on his. Oh, Lord, those gorgeous tits of hers with the incredibly tight nipples slid across his pecs. He frowned, attempting to process her words. She was giving him the verbal Dear John letter.

"I—" Words didn't come. Nothing came to mind other than her body rubbing against his.

"Do you have any regrets?" she repeated the question.

"Not a one. You?"

"No regrets. I'd do it over again given a second chance."

So the hell would he. "There's a *but* in there." He ran his fingers down her back, playing her like a classical guitar.

She ran a finger across his chin, tracing his lips, giving him mixed messages. He chose to follow the message her body was sending.

"You know, that *but*. The one that says *but* we can never do this again." Brody trapped her index finger between his teeth and sucked on it.

She blinked at him as if she'd forgotten what they were talking about. "I guess that would be a good idea. I mean, not to do this again." She slid her hand over his abs and wrapped her fingers around his cock. No mixed message there.

"Yeah, really good idea." He released her finger and sucked on her neck instead.

She rubbed her cheek against his stubbled chin. "Never. Going. To. Happen. Again." Her labored breathing told a different story as did the hand milking his cock.

"Never." He produced a condom from the stack on the nightstand and rolled it onto his painfully hard erection. Good thing he'd picked up a box at the pharmacy earlier. At this rate, they'd use every one of them in less than twenty-four hours. He pinned her on her back, grasped her ankles and spread her legs wide and high. The action opened her to him like a flower to a hummingbird, a very horny hummingbird after her sweet nectar. She was so wet for him, he slid deep in one long stroke.

"Oh, God." She tossed her head from side to side on the pillow. "I'm glad we're never doing this again."

"Yeah, me, too." He withdrew and thrust into her tight, wet heat. He picked up his rhythm, each thrust into a heaven he'd never experienced before. Judging by the way her fingernails dug into his back and passion lit her eyes, the feeling was mutual.

He bent down and took her mouth again; releasing her legs, he anchored his hands on either side of her face. Gazing into her eyes, he saw his future as clearly as he saw his past. She wrapped those shapely legs around his waist and encouraged him. He drove them higher, even as he drove deeper.

She clenched inside; her body tightened around his dick, creating the most incredible pressure, which sent him to the edge and catapulted him through the air. He never flew alone.

Mandy went with him, as she cried out his name. Together they flew through the air with wings constructed from their mutual passion.

Brody held her tight as they floated together in a place between fantasy and fiction. Afterward he sank into a blissful sleep with her even breathing feathering his shoulder.

* * * *

The strange noise, like a rusty Harley idling on her head, woke Mandy up from a sex-induced coma. Eyes still closed, she reached up and felt for the source of the noise. The answer came in the form of a fat belly and a handful of cat hair.

Turning, she came face to face with the blinking green eyes of Marlin. The cat smirked as if he knew things, too many things.

"How long have you been there?"

The cat purred louder, still smirking.

"You're a deviant little guy."

Marlin yawned and dug his claws into her shoulder. She pushed him away.

Brody lay sprawled on his back, arms and legs spread out to each side, bed hog extraordinaire. Wait until Mr. Neat-and-Tidy found out he was sharing a bed not only with her, but with Marlin and Sunny. Her blind dog took a cue from Brody and lay sprawled at the foot of the bed.

Males—didn't matter the species, they were all alike.

Marlin shifted his fat belly on the pillow, his tail switching in Brody's face. Brody swatted at the tail as if it were a pesky fly. Mandy giggled, waiting for Brody to wake up and have a fit. It didn't take long. He sneezed several times, batted at the tail again, and opened one eye.

Mandy held her hand over her mouth to keep from busting up.

Brody opened the other eye and squinted. *Smack*. Darn good aim right across the nose. Marlin crawled closer to him, rubbing up against his face.

"What the hell?" Brody shot up in bed, wiping cat hair off his face and glaring at Marlin. Unaffected, Marlin stood, planted his butt on Brody's still-warm pillow, turned a few circles, and lay down.

A giggle escaped Mandy's lips, followed by full-out, gut-stomping laughter. Brody scowled at the cat, the dog, and her. Then his ocean blue eyes turned warm. He scrubbed his face with his hands, threw back his head, and laughed as hard as she did.

Brody threw his arms around her and pulled her close to his warm, naked body. His chest shook and she laughed all the harder.

Until—

Oh, wow, morning wood. Really impressive morning wood. Her laughter faded and so did his. His mouth sought hers, and she didn't make her lips hard to find.

Only then in the morning light did something on the nightstand catch her eye. A picture of Frank stared at her, reminding her of all the reasons sleeping with Brody was a very bad idea.

Mandy wrenched away from Brody and stood beside the bed. Last night hadn't been about guilt and regrets, but this morning certainly was.

The weight of what she'd done crushed her, made it hard to breathe. She picked up the picture and turned it over.

Brody came up behind her and laced his fingers over her belly. "I know what you're feeling."

"Do you? Do you really?" She pulled out his arms and turned to face him. Only seconds earlier, his blue eyes had been lit with passion. Now disappointment dulled them. But disappointment at who? Both of them?

"Yeah, I do. We're really doing that regret thing now, aren't we?"

She nodded and grabbed a pillow off the bed to hold in front of her naked body, as much to keep space between them as to cover herself.

"Aww, honey, you can't live your life wallowing in memories. Frank's not alive anymore, but you are." He reached for her, but she batted his hand away.

"Don't touch me. You need to leave now. You don't understand."

Brody's hands fell to his sides. The hurt on his face almost made her re-think her decision, but she held strong. "But, Mandy."

"Get out, please. Just get out." A little hitch in her voice betrayed another crying jag welling up inside her.

He hesitated, but only briefly. Gathering his clothes, he walked to the door, shoulders squared, and didn't look back.

Mandy shoved her fist in her mouth, stuffing the sob back down her throat.

Chapter 14—Hot Fudge Sundaes

Friday came, and Brody's day just kept getting shittier. First, Mandy avoided him all day, obviously drowning in self-recrimination. Second, he battled his own demons regarding Frank and Frank's wishes for Mandy to find a nice guy. Third, he'd made the decision to deal with his problem quarterback. If you're going to make it rain, you might as well make it pour.

He stood in the locker room, attempting to push images of Mandy's luscious body from his mind and concentrate on Case's pre-game speech. Only every phrase Case uttered brought a sexual connotation to mind. *Give it everything you've got. Don't let up. Play hard and play loose. Ram it down their throats.* And Brody's personal favorite, *earn every inch.*

Damn. He put his clipboard in front of his pants, not happy to be thinking X-rated thoughts in a PG-rated situation. Mandy did that to him, even more so now because he'd sampled—more than sampled—the goods. They'd had sex soft and sweet and hard and raunchy. Mandy seemed to like it any way he dished it out. He sure as hell liked it any way she wanted to give it to him. Not that he'd be getting any more from her, even if she offered.

Idiot. Somewhere in heaven Frank shook a finger at him, admonishing him for thinking with his dick. Frank expected him to be a better guy than this. An honorable man never touched his dead buddy's widow, especially not after said buddy made it clear guys like Brody weren't the right guys for her.

Frank hadn't been the right guy either, but that hadn't stopped him. *And Brody, buddy, your point is?*

He didn't have a clue what his point was, other than to justify his unjustifiable actions. He shouldn't have slept with her last night, but given the chance, he'd do it over again.

How's that for being a stupid bastard?

The team stood and shuffled their way out of the locker room, pulling Brody back to the matter at hand. He motioned to Connor. "We need to talk."

Defiant and surly, Connor stopped and stared him down. The kid stood with his legs braced apart and his hands fisted at his sides, a challenging posture if Brody ever saw one. He'd teach the kid a thing or two about picking your battles. He stared right back. The kid hadn't learned a thing, even something as simple as the futility of taking on Brody in a staring match. His gaze unwavering, Brody narrowed his eyes and pinned the kid against the wall with his best bad-ass glare.

To his credit, Connor held his gaze longer than most but finally looked away. "What do you want?"

"You're not starting tonight."

"You can't do that. Let me talk to Coach." Connor stared at him in disbelief and turned to leave the room. Brody grabbed his arm and spun him back around. Judging by the uncertainty flashing across Connor's face, he didn't bargain on Brody being so strong.

"He knows about it. He agrees with me."

"No way. He'd never do that to me. He knows what a tool you are."

"Well, it appears he's agreed to be a tool, too, because you're benched. Call me a tool one more time, and I'll add another game."

Hatred mixed with frustration flashed in Connor's eyes. He threw his helmet across the locker room. It slammed against a metal locker, bounced, and rolled to bump Connor's toe. "Fuck you. I quit."

Brody raised one eyebrow, allowing that to be his only visible reaction. "Really? Is that how you handle adversity? You quit? I'd never pegged you for a quitter; shows how wrong I was."

"I'm not a quitter."

"Then what exactly do you call yourself? You just quit on

your team. Guys who depend on you, look up to you. You're the team's best chance at a championship. Hell, kid, I've played on championship teams before. One thing we all had in common is we wanted that championship so badly we could taste it. The desire to heft that trophy flowed through our veins. Every breath we took was dedicated to winning it. If you don't want it that badly, then this team doesn't need you." Brody stepped forward, and Connor backed up into the locker. Cornered, he didn't seem quite so brave.

"I want it, too." The kid almost sounded like he was going to cry, but he squared his jaw and jailed his emotions.

"Show me."

"How?"

"Stop being an arrogant asshole and learn what I have to teach you. You think you're so good that you can't improve your game?"

Connor stared at the floor and shook his head. "No, I never said that."

"What? I can't hear you. Speak up."

Connor lifted his head, a little of the defiance back in his eyes. "I never said that."

"You don't need to say it. You show it in your actions, your disrespect, your complete disinterest in learning a new technique." Brody stabbed his finger in Connor's chest. "You know what I see in you? I see me. Arrogant. Stupid. And willing to throw away a bright future because I know better than anyone."

"You think I have a bright future?" Connor met his gaze. Hostility still shone in his eyes, but a glimmer of something else gave Brody hope. The kid hid his vulnerability behind a mask of bravado.

"Yeah, if you're willing to put in the work. I can help you get a scholarship. Full-ride. To a Division 1 school. You're that good. Think about it." Turning, Brody headed for the door. He strode onto the football field, resisting the urge to look over his shoulder to see if Connor was following. He ignored the questioning stares of the team. Case slid closer to him but didn't say a word.

Brody called the backup quarterback over and ran through a few plays with him. The kid, only a sophomore, stared at him as if he couldn't comprehend a word his coach said. This wasn't going to be pretty. Not one damn bit.

The team took to the field. A few plays into the game, Case nudged him, jerking his head in the direction of the locker room. Connor, fully suited up, jogged to the sidelines, his helmet dangling from his fingers. Ignoring his coaches, he shouted encouragement to his teammates.

Brody breathed a sigh of relief. He turned slightly to look for Mandy in the stands. Their eyes met briefly. The concern in hers warmed his heart. He gave her a small smile. She nodded and gave him the thumbs up.

Brody re-focused on the field, only his brain stayed with Mandy. She'd supported his decision to bench Connor. Now she acknowledged his triumph. And her approval meant more to him than anything else in this world.

Brandon Siedel intercepted a pass and ran it back for a touchdown. Brody glanced at the scoreboard, as if he didn't have it committed to heart. Six to fourteen. Jackie Burt booted the extra point through the uprights. Three minutes left. The defense held the Tigers, and they punted.

Brody tapped Connor on the shoulder, and Connor turned to him, his face eager and hopeful. "You're in, kid."

"What do you need me to do, Coach?"

He'd never called Brody Coach before. Never. Brody's chest swelled with pride, like a proud papa whose son finally got it. Brody outlined the next play. Connor listened and nodded then he jammed on his helmet and ran onto the field.

Brody paced the sidelines in tandem with Case. He felt every hit Connor took. His body mirrored the moves Connor made on the field, as if he'd win the game for the quarterback.

A couple plays later, the team knocked on the door. Ten yards to the end zone and four chances to get there. Not bad odds in Brody's opinion. Connor jogged to the sidelines and waited for instructions. He inclined his head so he could hear his coach. Animated and talking with hands, his whole body and his mouth, Brody spoke to Connor, and Connor's head bobbed up and down. With a thumbs up, the kid sprinted back to the field.

The entire Wildcats crowd stood as one. The team strained to see the end zone from their spot on the sidelines. Connor stepped up to the line of scrimmage with his signature confidence and called the signals. Brody knew now the kid's confidence was a façade, like his had been. But at this point, it didn't matter, as long as the team believed in him, and they did.

Connor called the signals, stepped back, and looked for a wide-open receiver. Just as Brody had outlined the play, Bernie Wells shook off his defender and used his superior speed to get to the end zone several steps ahead of anyone else. Connor threw a perfect pass and Bernie caught it and hauled it in, scoring six points with five seconds to go. Thirteen to Fourteen.

Case motioned Brody over. "What's the play, Coach?"

Brody hid his surprise at being consulted with the game on the line. "I'd go for two, up the middle to Ethan or sidelines again to Bernie if he's open."

"Me, too."

Brody almost smiled. He might be starting to like this coaching gig.

Five seconds later, Connor, unable to find an open man, punched it into the end zone himself for two. They won the game by one point. Brody couldn't suppress the grin. Case slapped his back. The guys were all high-fiving each other. All the crap from earlier faded away. In fact, Brody felt pretty damn good, considering how shitty the day had started.

He followed his team to the locker room, searching the crowd for Mandy. She stood near the gate with Caro. His gaze met hers.

"Good game." Her wide smile warmed him from the inside out.

"Thanks." He hesitated. An overwhelming urge to engulf her in a victory hug surged through him. Case stepped up and stole his thunder by hugging his sister.

Brody backed away and headed for the locker room. The good feeling faded somewhat. Once more reality slapped him in the face. He didn't belong here, and he definitely didn't belong with Mandy.

She needed a good, stable man. That man wasn't him, and they both knew it.

* * * *

Mandy anxiously watched the door of the pizza place, wondering if Brody would show up for the after-game pizza ritual. Players, students, and parents packed the tables about the room. Caro stared at her as if she had something to say.

"You slept with him." Caro never held back for long.

Heat rushed to Mandy's face. "Him who?"

"Rick, who else? Did you fall asleep halfway through?" Caro rolled her eyes.

"I didn't sleep with Rick."

"Like duh. So how was he?"

"Rick?"

Caro blew out an exasperated breath, poured her second beer from the pitcher, and rolled her eyes. "Brody. Is he as hot as he looks?"

Hotter. Way hotter. "I have no idea what you're talking about."

"Yeah, I know, and your face isn't redder than that crap you put in your hummingbird feeder. Did you know red dye is bad for the birds?"

"No, I didn't know. Thanks for telling me."

"So is he good?"

"I think Brody's a good coach."

"Hmmm. As long as it's been, you probably needed some coaching."

Mandy battled with spilling her guts to her best friend and remaining in denial. "I'm a quick study when it comes to certain activities."

The look on Caro's face was priceless. "Way to go, girl. Now, don't go getting all guilt-ridden and crap on him. You have nothing to be sorry for or ashamed of. Got it? No regrets."

"Easy for you to say, but not me. Frank and I were supposed to grow old together."

"Well, guess what? You're not. Where does it say you can't have someone else in your life? Do you honestly believe Frank wouldn't want you to move on?"

Mandy couldn't answer that. At times Frank could be jealous and a little possessive. She didn't know what Frank would want. Except for the text message.

Mandy Lou, I'm sorry. Let go. It's time. FL

A chill slid down her spine. She'd put that strange message out of her mind, certain someone had played a very cruel joke on her. But who? And who knew Frank's nickname? Unless the initials stood for something else.

"Are you okay? You look like you've seen a ghost."

No, she hadn't exactly seen a ghost but a text message from one.

"Aw." Caro nodded, reading her mind in that uncanny way she had at times. "The message. Well, then I rest my case. He wants you to move on."

"But not with Brody. He is so out of here in another month or two."

"I wouldn't be so sure of that."

Mandy shook her head. She was sure of it. Brody craved the kind of excitement he couldn't get in this small town. Frank tried to be a stay-at-home husband on more than one occasion, but eventually he'd gotten bored and restless and off he'd go on another mission, each one more dangerous than the last.

"Don't look now, but here comes hot stuff."

Mandy did look, and she drank her fill. Brody stopped a few times to talk to kids and parents as he made his way across the room.

"I need to talk to you, Mr. Jenkins." Caro grabbed an empty chair and wedged it between her and Mandy. Across the table Case watched, his frown deepening. Brody dropped into the chair. His thigh rubbed against Mandy's. She looked down at the table and drew water rings with her glass. The steam rising off her should've been visible for any and all to see. She didn't dare look at Case. He'd figure it out in a second once he saw her face, as surely as if she'd written *I did it with Brody a dozen times last night* on her forehead.

Brody avoided her gaze, too. "So what's up?"

Caro launched into her armchair coaching routine. "Why did you bench my nephew? Was he hurt? What did he do? Case said to ask you about it."

Mandy chanced a look at Brody. His handsome face wore its usual unreadable mask. He outlined all the reasons why he benched Connor, ticking off each point on his fingers with logical precision even Caro couldn't argue against. In fact, she chose to drop it.

"Do you think you've come to an understanding with him?" Caro started on her third beer, while Brody drank a glass of water.

"To a point. A stubborn kid like him doesn't give up his opinions overnight. I know, I was like that."

"You still are." Caro always called it like it was.

Mandy choked on a laugh at the surprised expression on Brody's face. He turned his blue gaze on her and heat just about melted her body into a puddle on the floor.

"You *are* stubborn." She backed up her best friend.

"Yeah, so? And you aren't?"

Case decided to jump in on the conversation with his own unwanted brotherly opinion. "She's more stubborn than a mule in a carrot patch, as our grandfather used to say."

"He said that about you, not me, dear brother."

"I don't recall that."

"Of course, he doesn't. All men have selective memories," Caro said.

"So? That's how we manage to deal with the women in our lives when they nag the hell out of us over every stupid thing."

"And what woman in your life would that be?"

Mandy watched Case and Caro bicker with interest. They'd always fought like brother and sister, yet this seemed different with more of an edge to it. Definitely not like siblings. She'd never picked up on any kind of chemistry between them. Maybe the electricity radiating off of her and Brody had short-circuited their brains.

She met Brody's gaze. He smiled at her, a deep, warm, jump-into-bed-with-me-tonight smile. And she knew she would because despite every intention to keep hands off, she couldn't resist Brody any more than she could a hot fudge sundae or watching a Madrona sunset.

Chapter 15—Nip in the Air

In the next month, the leaves turned colors and fell from the trees. A nip in the air ushered in October, a change in seasons signaling a change in Brody's life.

Despite constantly recalling every conversation he'd had with Frank on the subject of Mandy, Brody couldn't keep his hands off her. Obviously, she couldn't keep her hands off him either. They'd fallen into bed together again and again, even though they both pledged that one night would be it. Over the next few weeks, they'd screwed each other's brains out night after night, like they were making up for lost time and banking even more hours for the future.

A future without Mandy. A future away from this small island where everybody knew everybody's business. Just the type of place Brody found smothering and boring as hell. At least he used to. Only he didn't feel smothered or bored. At least not yet. But then a guy would have to be a moron to be bored while enjoying Mandy's hot, curvy body every night.

They didn't discuss their feelings or their relationship, as if they both agreed to live in the moment. Mandy hadn't mentioned Frank in over a week, even though his pictures still stared accusingly at Brody from the fireplace mantle.

The house was coming along nicely, and Brody took great pride in his part. His masculine preferences were stamped on many of the rooms along with Mandy's feminine accents. He liked the contrast between the two; somehow they melded well.

Brody clenched a couple nails between his teeth and finished nailing up the shelving in the pantry off the kitchen. Thank God, Mandy had gone to church this morning with Caro so he could get some work done rather than staying in bed all morning.

Later they'd go to her family's house for Sunday dinner, like it was a routine thing for them to do together.

Together.

They weren't fooling anyone except themselves. Case's dirty looks had turned thoughtful, even if they were skeptical. Yet, so far he asked no questions. The other brothers butted out, always willing to let Case be the badass. Caro made no bones about her knowledge of their sordid affair but didn't pass judgment.

The door opened, and Case walked in without knocking.

Brody grunted at him as he carried a piece of trim out to the garage to cut it to length. Case followed him. "Shouldn't you be at church?"

"Nah, I leave that to women. Football on Sundays is the only church I need."

Brody could relate. He and Case were too much alike. He'd never been one to tolerate some pious preacher telling him how to behave, while the holy man did as he pleased. He realized his viewpoint on all things religious might be a little skewed. After all, he'd been the one to come home from school early and find his social-climbing mother going at it on the kitchen counter with the good reverend. Yeah, he'd never gone back to church since.

Brody steered the conversation to the one thing they could safely discuss. Somewhat. "Good game Friday night."

"Blew 'em out of the water. That's always a good game."

"Connor's not one-hundred percent with the program, but he's coming along."

"Time will tell." Case leaned against the workbench, arms over his chest, watching Brody. Brody let him brood, or whatever the hell the guy happened to be doing. He figured he'd get his ass chewed soon enough.

Case didn't disappoint. "You're sleeping with my sister."

"My sex life and your sister's are actually none of your business."

Case's eyes narrowed. The truce they'd establish the last few weeks disintegrated to dust. "Her happiness is my business. What are your intentions?"

Was this guy for real? Hell, he could make up something

that'd have Case on him so fast they'd be throwing punches like Ali and Fraser. Unfortunately, the truth would piss the guy off more than anything Brody made up. "I don't answer to you. Ask your sister since you seem to think you have some kind of control over her."

"Obviously I don't."

Brody shrugged and carried the lumber back into the house with Case hot on his heels.

"Are you still leaving in November?"

Brody positioned the trim on the floor and nailed it in place, wishing he could nail Case's mouth shut. "Why wouldn't I?"

"I thought—" Case hesitated, as if searching for words which eluded him. "I thought you liked it here. You like coaching?"

Brody sat back on his haunches and pretended to examine the trim. He couldn't be hearing this right. It almost sounded like Case wanted him to stay. "Yeah, I like coaching." More than he ever thought he would.

"This house is coming along pretty fast. You'll have it done in another month."

"Yeah, I'm ahead of schedule."

"Are you going to leave as soon as it's finished?"

Brody grabbed the side of the counter and rose to his feet. "I'm staying on until the season is over. I gave you my word, and I'll keep it."

"Except where my sister's concerned."

"Keep her out of this," Brody snapped at Case, even as he cringed inside. Maybe he hadn't given Case his word to leave Mandy alone, but he'd certainly given Frank his word, even if it happened after his death.

"You're a good coach. We could use you. Do you think you'll be back?"

Some part of Brody wanted to answer yes, which shocked the hell out of him. He stared out the window. "Looks like rain."

Case was quiet for a moment, then responded. "Yeah, the rain comes and goes around here this time of year. Never stays long."

"That's rain for you. You can't predict it, you can't control it, you just have to live with it."

"Maybe, but you can have enough sense to come in out of the rain when someone offers you shelter."

"If you're the type who likes your comforts."

Case regarded him with hooded eyes, not giving much away. "Yeah, I guess some of us seek shelter in a storm and some of us seek the storm." He looked like he might say something else. But he didn't. He walked to the door. "See you at Sunday dinner."

Brody stared after him long after he'd shut the door. A smart man would accept shelter rather than stand outside and get soaking wet down to his boxers.

Sometimes Brody questioned his own intelligence.

* * * *

Mandy ignored the curious stares of her family. Judging from their probing looks *I'm having mind-blowing sex with a hot guy* was spray-painted all over her face. She feigned ignorance and asserting control over her own life.

Aunt Kat passed the mashed potatoes, but they came with a price—her opinion. "It's good to see you looking happy again."

Mandy ducked her head to hide the all-too-familiar blush. "Getting this house finished lifts a huge weight off my shoulders."

"We'll plan a grand opening for the B&B." She could see the wheels already turning in her mother's head. She'd invite the entire island. Her mother turned to Brody, lining him up in her sights. "Brody, we're so thankful you came along when you did. You're such a savior to this family."

Brody's tanned face took on a deep red tinge. Her mother

could embarrass the toughest of men. Mandy witnessed it time and again; no wonder her mother never remarried. Even Frank had done her bidding.

Frank?

She hadn't thought of Frank once all day. Brody occupied her thoughts while the minister droned on about faith and forgiveness. In fact, looking back on the last few weeks, she didn't recall thinking much about her late husband at all.

She *should* feel guilty. She'd lived with the guilt and grief for so long, its absence should seem strange. Maybe she'd moved on. Finally.

No man would ever replace Frank as her first love. But Frank wouldn't have denied her a relationship. He'd never want her to be lonely for the rest of her life. It'd taken her three years to figure that out but finally she had. She wanted a future, maybe even kids and a man to warm her bed, to be her best friend, and one to take her out when she didn't feel like cooking, which happened to be most of the time.

Mandy wanted that man to be Brody.

If only she could convince him that small towns held excitement, too, just a different type of excitement. He liked it here, she could tell. His face had lost its stress lines. He hadn't woken her up with nightmares in a while. And the sex, well, the sex was fantastic.

She glanced over at him. With a neutral smile plastered on his face, he nodded his head as her aunt and mother grilled the poor man on everything from a leak in the bathroom to the high school football team. He answered their questions politely between bites of turkey and mashed potatoes. She could tell the man was almost having an orgasm over her mom and aunt's cooking; those women could cook.

Aunt Kat glanced at Mandy with a Caro grin. Mandy braced herself, fearing what might be coming next, as if Caro wasn't bad enough. "So Brody, you seem to be fitting in just fine on the island."

Brody stopped in mid chew, stared at her aunt, and

finished chewing his food before he answered. "It's a change of pace."

His totally non-committal answer didn't surprise Mandy one bit, but her mother and aunt weren't placated with his response.

"How do you like coaching? We've already booked our rooms in Tacoma for the state championship."

Brody winced. "We're progressing. We can't guarantee where we'll end up, but the kids are giving it all they've got. Right, Case?"

Case, who'd obviously been laying low and flying under the radar, looked up. "Uh, yeah, Mom, it's looking good. We even had a few college scouts at the last game checking out Connor." He glanced at Brody. "Thanks to Brody."

"I didn't do much. I had a few contacts, and I called them. Connor's talent speaks for itself."

Mandy glanced from her brother to her lover. Whoa, Case actually gave Brody some credit. She checked her watch. Nope. The earth hadn't stood still. Not yet, anyway.

Aunt Kat reached over and patted Brody's shoulder. "Regardless, dear, we love having you around. You're just the kick in the pants that island needs."

Her mother nodded vigorously. "Absolutely, Brody. Sunset Harbor needs more good people like you."

Brody stared at them, looking like a caged lion about to go on a rampage and bust out of his prison. "I—I—have a job to do. I need to report the middle of December, if not earlier."

"Mom, leave Brody alone. He'll do what he needs to do. Okay?" Mandy tried to call them off, but the two women had caught the scent of blood and nothing would stop them.

Case folded his napkin, crossed his arms over his chest, and watched, amusement flickering in his eyes. His brothers followed suit, all too willing to let the matriarchs of the family focus on the new guy. Meanwhile, Brody squirmed in his chair, while Mom and Aunt Kat moved in for the kill.

Mandy panicked, desperate to find a way to save the man

who shared her bed. By the time her family got through with him, he'd be ripping out of her driveway and never looking back. "Brody, we need to go if we're going to make the next ferry."

Brody narrowed his eyes and glanced up at her. Then he looked down at his plate heaped with food. Perhaps she'd misjudged him. Food might win out over rabid female relatives. "We do? Could I have a to-go box?"

Aunt Kat jumped to her feet, grabbed his plate, and hustled into the kitchen. A split second later she appeared with cellophane wrapped around his meal. "You kids hurry along and feed the animals. God forbid they miss a meal."

Mandy stared at her aunt like she'd gone crazy but gladly accepted the out. Brody stood at the same time she did. They said their goodbyes and slipped out the door.

Mandy settled in the passenger seat of Brody's SUV. "I'm sorry. They're a little overbearing."

Brody shrugged, started the engine, and drove out of the driveway. "No big deal."

"Are you sure?"

"Yeah."

"They want you to stay."

"I know. They're not pressuring you to sell the place either."

"No, they're not. Not right now."

They made small talk on the ferry, disembarked, and drove in silence down the windy, two-lane country road. In the distance a slash of glittering moonlight cut across a calm Chinook Channel. "Brody, you missed the driveway."

"I've always wondered where this road went." He stared straight ahead and drove until the road dead-ended at a small boat launch. He stopped and turned off the engine. He turned toward her, his face an emotionless mask.

Dread flowed through her veins as her heart pounded in her chest. She held her breath, waiting for the inevitable. He slid his arm across the back of the seat and tucked her against him.

"Gorgeous night." His strong jaw moved, as if wanting to say more but nothing would come out.

"It is." She leaned her head on his chest and closed her eyes, pretending they weren't the longshots in this race. They might be living in a fantasy, but it was her fantasy, and she'd live it as long as she could.

"Want to take a walk along the shore? The tide's out."

"Brody, I live on the water, we didn't have to drive out here to do that."

"Different view?" He grinned at her, looking like a teenager rather than a grown man.

"It is but not by much."

"Humor me." He opened the Jeep door, crossed around, and opened the door for her. Taking her hand, he helped her out.

"Wow, such a gentleman."

"I'm always a gentleman."

"And I've always been a size six."

His expression sobered quickly. "I like you fine. You're a lot sexier to me than a woman with a stick body."

"Well, I'm glad one man on this earth thinks so." Especially the only man who counted. Plus, she'd lost ten pounds on their morning walks. She'd definitely miss those walks, along with a lot of other things about him. She held onto this fragile relationship they'd developed, afraid to mention the elephant in the room for fear reality would shatter their fantasy. A month ago, that elephant would have been Frank, now not so. Instead it was Brody's imminent departure. Frank still hung over her, but not as strongly. Brody had healed a lot of those wounds, given her something to live for, showed her she could live again, even if she might not love again and have it returned.

"I got a call from my boss today."

"Oh." She couldn't think of a single other thing to say.

"They need me, but I told them I couldn't let the team

down. I promised I'd stay until their season ends."

"The kids will be glad. So will Case." Mandy wanted to ask, "What about me? What about staying here with me?" She turned her head away from him as he led her down the path to the water.

"I'm not so sure about Case, though we seem to have developed a mutual tolerance for each other."

"You're not threatening to beat each other to a pulp anymore."

"Not so much."

"Connor's coming along. Caro said he doesn't call you an asshole anymore, just a jerk."

"I've risen in his eyes." Brody chuckled.

"You're risen in a lot of people's eyes."

He shrugged. "Yeah, maybe. They aren't threatening to run me out in the dark of night."

"They never were. You've made an impact here."

He stared out over the water, her hand loosely held in his. "It's been an experience I won't forget."

Neither would she. She'd never forget him. "Do you think you'll be back?"

"No, it's best that way."

Mandy swallowed hard and forced her expression to remain neutral. "How about we not dwell on the future, and just enjoy the next month together. No regrets, no expectations past the thirty days. How's that sound to you?"

"Sounds great." His flat tone of voice didn't mirror his words.

"I'm cold. Let's get home. I need to feed the animals."

Brody nodded, and Mandy led the way back to the Jeep, anxious to forget about this conversation and jump into bed, the one place she could forget Brody's temporary status in her life, even if only for a short while.

Chapter 16—On the Offense

Brody cupped his hands to his mouth and yelled at the offensive line to close up and protect the quarterback. He'd worn a path in the strip of grass right in front of the bench with his nervous pacing.

Nervous? Brody never showed outward signs of nerves, no matter how dire the situation until now. And for a high school football game? Not exactly a life-threatening situation. Yet he felt as invested in coaching as he would have with his life on the line. Go figure.

Case nudged his elbow. "You'd think we were losing by thirty points instead of winning by thirty. Calm down before you burst a major blood vessel and have a stroke."

Brody ignored Case and shouted a few more instructions. If the team won, they'd be in the playoffs. The clock ticked down, and the final buzzer sounded. The crowd cheered as the kids ran off the field. Brody moved forward to slap backs and dole out words of praise. Connor slipped past him, cunningly placing his body on the other side of the Wildcats' biggest lineman. A slight twinge of pain tweaked Brody's heart. He ignored it. He might have achieved a coldly professional working relationship with Connor, but the kid didn't like him much. In fact, the dislike vibrated off him in waves, even though he grudgingly did everything Brody requested.

But, hell, coaching wasn't a popularity contest. Brody had three goals, One—to make these boys better young men by teaching them values such as hard work. Two—to give them a taste of teamwork. Three—to drive home that anything is possible if you just believe. After all, football was as much mental as physical. Brody knew that better than anyone.

Brody wasn't sure he practiced what he preached, but the kids didn't need to know that. He didn't believe he deserved the same things other guys got and took for granted, like a home, a family, a place he belonged. The only two places he'd ever felt at home were on a football field and in the Army. If he allowed himself to be honest, perhaps he felt a little bit at home on Madrona Island, and in the house he'd left his mark on to the point where he secretly considered it his home.

He shook his head but nothing cleared the thoughts pinging off each other like the balls in a lottery drawing. He knew the answer to that question already; maybe that's why he never settled down. As a moving target, he never had to reflect on where he was and how he'd gotten there, never took responsibility for anyone but himself and his fellow soldiers.

Brody raked a hand through his unruly hair, which had grown too long for his taste, much to his surprise. He couldn't recall his last haircut, which shocked him. He remembered things like getting a haircut with clockwork precision. God forbid if some of Mandy's messy ways rubbed off on him.

The kids jogged into the locker room and he followed, scanning the crowd for Mandy. The entire town must have turned out for this game. He couldn't find her anywhere. Pushing his way through the people, he nodded his head as everyone sought a piece of him. Words of congratulation swirled around him from every direction. He'd never been much for crowds. Once he'd come back from the first tour, he liked them even less. Abandoning his mission to find Mandy, he did an about face, and shoved his way past a wall of people, ignoring their annoyed stares.

He didn't mean to be rude, but the claustrophobia clawed at him until escape became his priority. A knot of panic tied itself around his normally rational brain. He fought to keep it under control all the while displaying outward calm. Thank God it was a small town and small school. It didn't take much to get free of the crowd, such as it was. Brody slipped through the gate in the chain link fence surrounding the field and walked around the corner of the building. He stopped there, his chest heaving and his hands shaking. He heart slammed against his rib cage as if it was trying to find a way to escape. He wiped the cold sweat off his brow with sleeve of his heavy coat.

Crap.

Stuff like this didn't happen often. Usually he avoided situations that put him at risk, like being caught in the middle of a crowd, however small. He'd been caught off guard when the relatively small crowd surged toward him and the players.

A hand touched his arm, and he almost jumped out of his skin. He whirled around, ready to confront the enemy.

"Brody." Mandy's voice trembled with alarm and concern. Her half-raised hand froze in mid-air.

He backed up a few steps, alarmed at the fear on her face, and interpreting it as fear toward him. He most likely looked a little wild-eyed and on the verge of losing control. Instead of retreating, she came toward him and wrapped her arms around his waist.

"Are you okay?" She gazed up at him.

He stiffened and looked over the top of her head, his hands clenched at his sides, and his body trembling ever so slightly. She didn't back off like most women; instead she held him tighter. His body unwound like toilet paper rolling down a gentle slope. He rested his fingers on her hips and his chin on the top of her head. Brody drew in a few cleansing breaths and loosely weaved his fingers together behind her back. His breathing slowed and his heart stopped pounding.

Moving his head, he pressed his cheek against hers. "I'm okay." He spoke into her hair, letting it muffle his voice.

"I'm glad." She didn't press him for an explanation, and his heart softened at her attempt to keep his pride intact. She leaned back and wrapped her arms around his neck. After planting a messy, wet kiss on his lips, she smiled. "You'd better get to the locker room before you're missed."

He nodded, knowing she was right, even though he'd prefer to stay right where he was. "Yeah, see you at the pizza place in a few?"

"Wouldn't miss it."

Neither would he.

"I'll be with you every step of the way."

He gripped her hand, taking his strength from her and walked hand-in-hand with her back toward the crowd. As they surged around him, trying to get a piece of him, he held on to his lifeline.

* * * *

Mandy sat in a booth at the pizza place with Caro, who couldn't stop glancing at her watch and then at the door. Her friend had it bad for Case. In fact, come to think of it, she'd most likely harbored a crush on him for years, which explained their mutual dislike, which wasn't dislike at all. Whatever went on between the two—or didn't go on—she had enough problems to deal with; she didn't need theirs, too.

Mandy stirred her Pepsi with a straw and stared at the door. The team started to drift in the door, filling most of the tables, along with family and classmates. Connor came over to talk to his aunt, his face lit up and animated. A cute little cheerleader, different from the last girl Mandy had seen him with, slid up beside him. Connor hooked an arm over her shoulders, trying to look cool and detached, even though his eyes sparkled when he looked at her. Oh, young love. So quick to fall in love and quicker to fall out of love.

Mandy's thoughts did a slingshot back to Brody. She'd seen him practically part the crowd with his bare hands earlier as if desperate to get away. Mandy knew that look. She'd seen it once on Frank, even though he'd refused to talk about it. Frank hadn't liked crowds either, said it came with the territory. Obviously the same territory in which Brody lived.

Yet Mandy was making headway with him. Instinctively, she knew he needed her as much as she needed him. Maybe, just maybe, it'd be enough, and he'd stay. Despite the trials, Brody loved coaching; he couldn't disguise his passion. Mandy liked to think he held a certain fondness for her, too. Sure he chided her about her casual attitude toward tidiness, but she'd improved over the past few weeks, not to his standards, but better than her previous efforts.

She'd grown used to him in her bed every night, along with Sunny and Marlin. Brody pretended to merely tolerate the animals, but she'd caught him talking to Marlin as the cat sat in his lap. The man hid a soft heart under a hard exterior.

In less than a month, the season would end, even if they took it all the way to the championship, and Brody would leave. Mandy shoved such depressing thoughts from her mind. She couldn't think about it. She'd live in the moment, enjoy what they had for as long as they had it. She'd be glad for the gift he'd given her—the gift of healing.

A familiar deep, hearty laugh caught her attention. Brody walked through the door, laughing and joking with her brother and the other coaches. His gaze found hers and a slow, easy smile crossed his face. Her heart danced a waltz right to him, while her head insisted the man might be the best thing that happened to her in the past few years.

Mandy fell a little in love with him, with his rugged and ready half smile and pale blue eyes. Okay, who was she kidding? Maybe more than a little. Maybe a hell of a lot in love with him. Yeah, she'd known it for a very long time, but seeing him so comfortable with her brother, talking to the kids as he ordered pizzas, and fitting in as if he'd always lived here sealed her fate. She'd given her heart to another man with a hankering for danger.

And guess what? Right this minute and the next month full of minutes, she didn't give a damn. Not one bit.

Brody was hers. For now.

He settled into the seat next to hers and grinned at her. "Thanks for earlier."

"You're welcome."

"I thought you'd be afraid of me, but you weren't. I think you get it."

"As best as I can when I haven't been where you've been or felt what you feel."

He shrugged and sipped on his root beer. Brody never

drank in front of the team. Case slid into the seat next to Caro. She lit up like the town Christmas tree on Christmas Eve. Brody raised one eyebrow at Mandy. She nodded her agreement.

Under the table, he squeezed her hand. Mandy melted at his feet and swore she'd never stand again. They locked gazes. Brody's burned with desire. Yet hidden behind the desire, she saw a spark of something else, something she couldn't explain yet it gave her hope, hope that they might—just might—have a future.

Chapter 17—Touch Me Like That

After practice, Brody stood in the high school parking lot and debated. He could go back to the house and work on the tile floor, or he could go to the club for a beer. Mandy worked tonight, and he didn't like going home to an empty house.

Home? A chill ran through him. He didn't know when he'd started thinking of the house as his home, his and Mandy's. The realization struck a nerve, the same one that overreacted to tight, confining places and commitment. Yet he'd committed on some level to Mandy and this island in ways he'd never committed to anything but his defunct football and Army careers.

He slept in her bed every night.

Brody dragged his feet getting the house done. With so little left, he could complete it in a few days, yet if he did and the team lost their next game, he'd be out of reasons to stay.

He didn't want to be out of reasons to stay.

The security contractor didn't expect him back until the first week of December. He still had a month. *Almost.*

Brody prided himself on being a man who made cold, rational decisions. Lately his decisions bordered on emotional and irrational, at least to him. The sooner Brody left Madrona Island behind, the sooner he'd be back in his comfort zone, but he was also a man who honored his commitments. He'd made one to the team, and he'd see it through. Not because he had to but because he wanted to. Actually, he wanted to do a lot, and he was better off not exploring those want-to's too deeply.

Brody got in his truck and drove to the club. Once inside, he sat on his favorite barstool and watched his favorite bartender mix drinks and take orders with amazing efficiency for one so disorganized. Organized chaos. That was his Mandy.

Brody bit down on his lip until he tasted blood. She wasn't his. She never would be. Frank would always hold that place in her heart. Brody was just a convenient, temporary replacement. A smart man never forgot that.

Lately he'd begun to question his intelligence.

Case sat down next to him, and Brody stiffened, waiting for another lecture. Mandy slipped a beer across to him and gave Brody another then hustled off across the room.

"Great game, coach."

"Yeah. You, too." Brody studied his beer, refusing to look at Case and encourage more conversation.

"My sister is happier than I've seen her in a long time."

Brody grunted. Oh, crap, he knew where this was heading. He watched Mandy as she paused in front of table and listened to one of the old veterans tell a joke. She laughed on cue. Brody loved her laugh, loved her smile, and loved her kindness.

"Hey." Case snapped a finger in front of his face. "Wake up, man."

Brody jerked his head toward Mandy's brother. He felt the heat rise up to his ears. "Uh, sorry. I was watching the game."

Case looked at the TV. "What game?"

Busted. Brody didn't have an answer for that.

"You know, when a guy puts a smile like that on Mandy's face, a brother has to like him. To tell the truth, I don't think her husband ever put that kind of smile on her face, at least not the last five years of their marriage."

"You mean it wasn't perfect?"

"Hardly."

"Reality is a funny thing."

"Yeah, sure is. Especially when a person creates a reality which might not be fact." Case nodded toward Mandy. "A smart guy would value the affections of a woman like my sister."

"A smart guy would." Brody couldn't argue that fact. Only he didn't consider himself a smart guy. Not by a longshot.

Case drained the last of his beer, left a five on the bar, and stood. "I like you, Brody Jensen. Don't fuck this up." He strode out the door without another word, leaving Brody to stare after him with an open mouth.

"What did my brother say to you?"

Brody closed his mouth, composed himself, and turned to Mandy. "Uh, just talking about the game."

She looked as if she didn't believe him. He wouldn't have believed himself either. Hell, he didn't know what to believe anymore. She'd turned his life upside down and inside out.

He could stay. He didn't have to go. This could be his home, the place he made his future. How long would it take the claustrophobia to set in, to put him into a panic, and send him running back to his comfortable danger?

And how would she feel about him if he told her about his connection to Frank?

* * * *

Mandy opened her eyes and stared into the darkness and listened to Brody's steady breathing. She gave herself an "atta girl" since he hadn't had a nightmare since they'd been sharing the same bed.

The moon reflected off the water outside and made it somewhat easy to see in the dark. Mandy scooted up and leaned against the headboard. Brody lay sprawled on his back, his arms and legs out to the sides like the points of a compass. Mandy smiled as she gazed at this ruggedly handsome man. Definitely a man's man, a guy with deep convictions and deep secrets. Things he held inside because he didn't dare let them see the light of day. She couldn't pretend to know the horrors a guy like him might have seen. Frank had refused to talk about his missions, and Brody also kept his silence. Yet at least for a little while, she'd given him peace in his life, and he'd given her back her ability to love. She'd never be able to thank him enough because he couldn't know. If he stayed, it needed to be on his terms, not because he felt obligated to her. No, she wouldn't tell him, at least not with words.

Earlier that night the Wildcats won their quarterfinal game. Three games away from winning the state championship. Three very long games in which anything could happen.

Brody rode the bus home with the kids and the coaches. Mandy drove home with Caro, her mother, and aunt. Brody came dragging in the door, his limp more pronounced than she'd ever seen it. Despite his weariness, the smug set of his jaw revealed a man immensely pleased with himself. After stripping off his clothes, he fell into bed, exhausted—most likely emotionally more than physically. She cuddled next to him, and he started snoring in less than sixty seconds. Mandy fell into her own deep, contented sleep.

Until the cat woke her at four-thirty AM.

Now she couldn't fall back asleep. Good thing Brody slept like a rock, or she'd be keeping him awake with all her tossing and turning.

The wind rattled the windows and an eerie, unearthly howl reverberated through the dark room. Shivering, Mandy cuddled close to Brody, seeking the warmth of his big body.

He rolled over and pulled her into his arms.

"I thought you were asleep."

"I was."

"Well, now that you're awake…" She slid her hand between them, across his flat belly, and found what she was looking for. "You're definitely awake."

"Doesn't take much when you touch me like that."

Mandy ran her hand up and down the length of his erection. "Would you like me to stop?"

"Hell, no. You're killing me, woman." He groaned as she clutched him in her hand and squeezed.

"I thought you were tired." She hooked a leg over his hip and pressed against him.

"Exhausted." He flipped her onto her back and moved between her thighs. He pressed his cock into the wet opening, bypassing the foreplay with her blessing.

"That's what I thought. Barely able to lift a finger."

"Not one finger." With one strong stroke, he buried himself inside her with a strangled groan.

"I'm glad you're not lifting a, uh, finger. Please keep resting." That one stroke stole the breath from her lungs. The next stroke rendered her senseless and turned her brain into a worthless pile of matter. She wrapped her legs around his waist and held on for the ride of her life.

He began to thrust in and out with an enthusiasm which belied his claims of being tired. "Am I resting enough for you?"

"You could rest a little more, if you'd like."

Brody reared back and stared at her. She smiled up at him and squeezed his waist tighter with her legs. He thrust deep and high, leaving her screaming for mercy. She'd never been much of a screamer until now. Dang, she raised the roof off the house with her hollering. "I love a woman who lets her preferences be known."

"What. Are. My. Preferences." She panted each word as if it might be her last.

He froze in mid-stroke. "Ah, crap. No condom." As if it was killing him, he slowly withdrew.

"One moment please, hold that thought." Mandy yanked the nightstand drawer open with one hand, fumbled for a condom packet, ripped it open with her teeth, and sheathed him in record time. He sank back inside her with a satisfied sigh. He wasn't the only one who was satisfied. He filled her in ways beyond the physical, ways she'd never imagined in her wildest dreams.

Several more hard thrusts, and she blasted off. So did Brody. Together they left the ozone for the erotic zone. Mandy stared into his eyes and saw her future. Somehow she'd burrowed into his head, knew his thoughts, his wants, his needs. She saw the man she'd grow old with and the man who'd father her children. It was right. It was meant to be.

As she settled back into the sheets and sanity slowly returned, she wondered how the hell she'd convince Brody.

Chapter 18—Champions

Mandy slid a beer across the bar to Caro. Instead of taking a big swig, Caro ignored the cold brew and studied her with an eagle eye. "So spill, woman, you've been brooding a lot lately."

Mandy looked away and considered her options: lie or tell the truth or something in between. She made a futile attempt at lying, so not her forte. "I'm worried about the game on Friday."

"Sure you are. So where's the second hunkiest coach on the team?"

Mandy breathed a sigh of relief and gladly took the side road Caro offered. "My brother is meeting with Brody and the other coaches to watch game film."

"Sounds like a good excuse to drink beer." Caro rolled her eyes and tossed back her long black hair. "So what's really on your mind? You've been a drag lately."

"Well, thanks, I can't help but wilt when I'm eclipsed in the shadow of your brilliance."

"Then don't stand too close." Caro blinked a few times and stared at her beer, as if seeing it for the first time. She wrapped her fingers around the cold bottle, raised it to her lips, and took a long drink. Lowering the bottle, she sighed, as if in heaven. "Nothing like a good beer."

"New one from a microbrew on San Juan Island."

Caro lifted her cell phone and took a picture of the bottle. Mandy frowned at her but decided not to even ask. The crazy inner workings of Caro's mind were best left a mystery.

Instead she blurted out the words which had sat on the tip of her tongue all night. "The house is done."

"When's the celebration? I love a good party."

"I'm not having one, not without Brody."

"So have one with Brody. The place looks fantastic, and you're actually keeping it clean."

Mandy had to smile at that. "Well, not clean enough for

Brody's standards but clean for mine."

"Whatever. That's hardly enough to drive him away."

"Win or lose, Brody's leaving after the championship. In fact, he's not coming back to town afterwards. He'll leave straight from Tacoma."

"What? And miss the big celebration after we win the championship trophy?"

"That's what he says."

Caro adopted her old sage expression. "He's afraid if he comes back he won't leave."

"I suppose." A lump formed in Mandy's throat, and tears filled her eyes. Darn it. She didn't want to cry. She looked up at her friend. The sympathy on Caro's face undid Mandy. Thank God the place was empty.

"You don't want him to go."

"Of course I don't want him to go." Irritation crept into her voice. What a stupid-assed comment. From Caro of all people. "I'm in love with him."

"I know. Everyone knows. I'm guessing Brody knows, which is why he's going to run off like a chickenshit as soon as the last down is played."

Mandy sniffled and tried to control her on-the-edge emotions. "I'm going to lose another man I love. This is almost worse because it doesn't have to be this way."

"A brave women would throw caution to the wind, rip off her target's clothes, and keep him in bed for twenty-four hours straight. He won't be able to walk, let alone leave. In fact, he won't remember why he even wanted to leave."

"Easy for you to say. You're a screw-his-brains-out type of woman."

"I'll take that as a compliment."

"I know you will, no matter how it was meant." Mandy took the empty bottle from Caro, popped the top off another, and handed it to her friend.

"Pretend you're me. Convince him that this is where he belongs."

"I've been trying. I thought he was caving, but he's a tough guy."

"With a tender heart. He needs you more than you need him."

Mandy shook her head, puzzling over why the heck Caro would think such a thing. Brody Jensen didn't need anyone but Brody.

* * * *

Brody wiped his sweaty palms on his pants. The Tacoma Dome might not be filled to capacity, but the fans made up for it in sheer enthusiasm. Both sides of the stands rocked with townspeople and students from the rival teams, along with other interested spectators. Brody stood back and took it all in. He'd played in packed stadiums in his short college career, but strangely nothing equaled the electricity crackling around him. Some of the kids looked a little gray, while others bounced on the balls of their feet or jogged in place. Connor stared at the field with steely-eyed determination, as if visualizing his next touchdown, just as Brody had tried to teach him.

Brody turned and found Mandy in the first row behind the bench with family and Caro gathered around her. Her encouraging smile lit up his heart. Glancing around to make sure he wasn't needed, he slipped away from the team and leaned against the railing separating the stands from the field. Mandy leaned down, her smile growing wider.

"A kiss for good luck?" He grinned back at her, knowing he looked like a lovesick fool in the eagle eyes of friends and family.

She planted a big, wet one on his lips. He grabbed her hand and squeezed it. For some reason he just knew everything was going to be okay, win or lose, because with Mandy by his side he'd never lose.

Brody returned to the team, his step lighter and more confident. The team battled nerves the first half of the game but managed to stay within a touchdown at seven to fourteen. The Roseville Bulldogs were a tough team with a couple top-notch players. They intercepted Connor once when he forgot all Brody had taught him and forced the ball to his favorite receiver.

Case delivered a rousing halftime speech which had the entire team jacked up and ready for battle. Brody snagged Connor before the kid stepped through the tunnel onto the field. Connor looked at him with expectation rather than contempt, which was a first.

"Look, kid, you can do this. Just take a deep breath, relax, and remember everything I taught you. Most of all, go out there and have fun."

Connor didn't look like fun was even in his vocabulary. He looked nervous as hell. The kid glanced behind Brody. "Sid says there're college scouts here."

"Most likely, but they aren't your concern. Leading your team is your concern."

"Yes, sir." Connor managed a nervous smile and a snappy salute.

Brody slapped him on the back. "I'm proud of you."

Connor looked away, jammed his helmet on his head, and ran onto the field. Brody wished he could be out there. Standing helpless on the sidelines drove him nuts. He was a man of action, yet he also took a certain pride in the team he'd helped mold. These boys were good young men, and Brody took a measure of credit for that. Not only were they good football players, but they were good kids, decent students, and upstanding citizens. He'd tried to give them a better base than he'd had as a high school player. It wasn't all about the winning.

Oddly enough, Case and Brody agreed on that point. Few if any of these boys would have a career in football, so football needed to be used to build character and teamwork even in adversity.

Brody watched the offense march down the field and tie

the game. He leapt in the air, pumping his fist, yelling and screaming with the rest of the jacked-up crowd, coaches, and players. Damn, but he loved football. He was going to miss coaching more than he'd ever imagined.

The Wildcats scored again in the last minute. The clock ticked down and the Bulldogs made one last attempt to score but missed. The game was over. As the place erupted into bedlam, Brody stood silent for a moment. Two conflicting emotions warred inside him—elation over achieving their goal and having a part in it all and sorrow because it was over. He'd never coach these kids again, never debate the merits of certain plays with Case, never watch this small town rally around the kids and accept Brody as one of their own.

A shock of cold liquid drenched Brody's head and ran down his face, soaking his clothes. Brody whirled around to murder the perpetrators. Several of his offensive players laughed their collective asses off. Connor held the empty container in his hands and laughed harder than anyone. Nearby, Case had been equally soaked by the defense. Brody took a towel and wiped the sticky crap off his face, grateful for a change of clothes waiting for him in the locker room. Mandy came running toward him and threw her arms around him. Obviously, she didn't mind getting sticky. He lifted her in his arms and twirled her around, ignoring the pain shooting up his leg and the crowd gathering around.

Most of all, he wanted to share this moment with Mandy.

Brody Jensen had fallen in love—crazily, madly, passionately in love—possibly for the first time in his entire life. He didn't have a clue what the hell to do about it.

* * * *

Brody wrapped his arm around Mandy as they walked out of the stadium together. A dark figure stepped out of the shadows to stand in their path. Brody stepped in front of Mandy, pushing her behind him, alert and ready to protect, just like he'd been trained. Every muscle in his body bunched and prepared for action.

"Coach, could I talk to you?"

Brody unfisted his fingers, breathed a deep breath, and forced himself to stand down. "What's up, Connor?"

The kid stepped into the street light. His hair, still wet from the shower, stuck to his head. His cheerleader girlfriend hovered a few steps behind him. "I need to talk to you." Connor glanced behind him. "Alone."

Brody turned to Mandy. "Is that okay?"

Mandy nodded. "Sure, Brenna and I will wait over there." She indicated a spot several cars away under the next street light.

Brody waited until the women walked away. Keeping one eye on them, he turned to Connor. "Yeah?"

Connor looked past him at some unseen object in the distance. He worked his jaw, swallowed, and wrung his hands. Finally, he raked his fingers through his black hair. "Sometimes a guy is so stubborn he can't see what's best."

"Yeah, I've lived that story." Brody lounged against the hood of a car, feigning disinterest.

"Me, too."

"No shit?"

"No shit." Connor kicked at a rock with his shoe and watched it bounce across the parking lot.

"You played a good game."

Connor finally lifted his eyes to meet Brody's gaze. "Thanks to you."

"Nope, you're the one throwing the ball, calling the plays, taking the hits." This was Connor's moment of glory and Brody didn't want his share.

"You believed in me." Connor looked amazed.

"Yeah."

"Scouts are contacting Aunt Caro. I might get a full ride to college depending on how it goes my senior year."

"You're good enough."

Connor looked down again. "I don't know if I can do it alone."

Brody's heart clenched. "You won't be alone. You've got a big support group."

"Will I have you?" Connor met his gaze with a steady one of his own.

Brody hesitated, unsure how to answer that even though the inevitable answer sat poised on his tongue. "I'm leaving. I have a job to do. They expect me to report in a few days."

"Aunt Caro says you can quit. You don't have to go. If we meant something to you, you'd stay."

"It's not that, buddy. Seriously. I need to go back. It's my responsibility."

"You don't feel responsible for us? You don't think we need you?"

Brody's mouth dropped open. Connor's words rendered him speechless. Only a few people had ever needed him in his entire life. "You'll be fine."

"You're leaving us. Just like that. You really don't care, do you? It's all bullshit. You're walking away just like every other adult in my life." Connor spun away, stalked to his girlfriend, grabbed her arm, and disappeared into the darkness.

Brody stood rooted to the ground, a jumble of feelings bashing against each other in his brain. Mandy touched his shoulder. He jumped, caught off guard that she'd snuck up on him, and he hadn't noticed. "Are you okay?"

"Uh, yeah. Sure. Fine."

She didn't look convinced but didn't push it. "So what time are you leaving in the morning?"

"I'm going back to the island first. I'll pack up my stuff, got a few minor details to finish on the house, then I'll be gone in a few days." The words slipped out before he could stop them. He couldn't say goodbye yet.

"Oh, I thought you were leaving directly from here."

"My plans changed." What a liar. He'd had every intention of leaving tomorrow, but he couldn't. He'd prolong the inevitable. He'd dig up a few more things to finish on the house and spend a couple more nights in bed with Mandy. Then that'd be it. Then he'd be gone. Forever.

Staying was not an option. He didn't put down roots, he didn't stay in one place long. He'd get restless for the danger, the adrenaline rush, and he'd leave her broken-hearted. Even worse, if they tried to make a go of it, someday she might have to answer that knock on the door, and a perfect stranger would tell her she'd lost another man to war. He couldn't do that to her.

He'd given her back her life, by teaching her there was life after Frank. Now he had to give her the freedom to live it, even if it broke her heart in the short term.

And him?

His life would never be the same.

Chapter 19—Heartbreak

Mandy stared at the gorgeous kitchen, which had Brody written all over it. From the granite countertops to the rich wood cabinets and custom backsplash, every inch of it reflected Brody's painstaking pursuit of perfection and the loving care he'd put into her entire house.

Their house. Hers and Brody's.

Anyone could see Brody was dragging his feet over leaving. The house was done, and yet he created new jobs, such as a built-in cabinet in the garage to store tools and some unnecessary repairs on the garage.

They went to dinner at her mother's on Sunday. On Wednesday they attended the state championship celebration at the local community center. Brody handled the crowd pretty well. He stayed by Mandy's side all night long. Friday night the coaches and her brothers took him out for pizza. Not once did he mention leaving.

Maybe, just maybe he'd changed his mind.

Brody needed to know how she felt about him without her actually saying the words. Mandy knew just the gift, the sacrifice that she'd give to him.

She carried a box to the mantle and put it down. She stared at the multitude of pictures, every one of them. She picked up the one of Frank looking handsome in his uniform. A sad smile crossed her face, but the heart-wrenching pain didn't come. Not that his loss didn't hurt, but the gaping hole in her heart had shrunk to a small puncture wound. Still there, still with a dull pain, but nothing she couldn't live with and nothing to prevent her from feeling good about her future and herself. A small smile tugged at the corners of her mouth.

She gently kissed the picture, wrapped it in newspaper, and placed it in the box. "Goodbye, Frank. Part of me will always love you, but it's time." One by one she stowed the pictures in the box and sealed it. She walked around the house and boxed up the remainder of Frank's things and carried them to the garage to be stored. After that she boxed his clothes and took them to the car to be delivered to the church for their fall charity bazaar.

Coming back in the house, she stared at the empty mantle. Slowly she turned a circle in the finished living room with the rustic hardwood floors and matching trim. The house looked incredible. In fact, she'd even managed to keep it somewhat tidy. Maybe not Brody-tidy, but certainly tidier than she'd ever been in the past.

Frank was gone, but Brody remained, and she was confident he'd stay with a little nudge in the right direction. From what little he shared about his personal life, the man hadn't put down roots anywhere.

Madrona Island might be the best place to start.

* * * *

Something was different, something other than the rare smell of dinner in the oven. Brody took in the table set for two, the lit candlesticks, the muted lighting. Romance at its finest. Scanning the room with the same careful precision he used to scan the Afghan horizon for the enemy, Brody's gaze stalled out at the fireplace mantle.

He went still. His lungs stopped taking in oxygen. His heart stopped pumping blood. His head ceased to process information. Only for a split second, yet it seemed like an eternity. Then the smothering claustrophobia set in, crushing him, bearing down on him, making it even harder to breathe. He ran a hand over his face, but it didn't change the scene before him.

He sensed Mandy close behind him. She cleared her throat.

"The pictures are gone." His voice sounded strangled to his ears. Did it to hers?

"I did it today." She put her arms around him from behind. "Frank needs to be put away with the rest of the memories. I can't live with a ghost anymore. It's our house."

Our house? He couldn't even speak the words out loud.

"Oh, man. I knew this was a bad idea from Day One." Yeah, from the moment he'd looked into her kind brown eyes, seen the sadness there, and longed to be the one to make her smile. From the moment his cock stiffened at the sight of her curvy body and pretty face. From the moment they'd taken that first walk, and from the moment she'd awakened him from a nightmare.

"Maybe our hearts knew better than our heads." She moved to stand in front of him and looked him in the eyes.

"Our hearts don't know jack." He glanced away, afraid she'd see the truth there, the truth he'd only recently acknowledged. "I can't stay, you know?"

No, she didn't know. "Why can't you stay?"

"I can't." He couldn't hold the mask in place anymore; it shattered, and unleashed an entire array of conflicted, torn emotions.

"I love you, Brody Jensen." A tear left a track down her cheek, and his heart ached for what he had to do.

"I love you, too, Mandy."

"Then why aren't you staying?" Hope lit a smile on her face. The smile he was about to crush with his next words.

He led her to the couch and sat down with her, facing her, and holding her hands. Her brow furrowed with puzzlement. "What is it?"

"I haven't been straight with you."

Mandy sat back and frowned. "Whatever do you mean?"

"I knew Frank." There, he'd said the words that'd been plaguing him since he arrived.

"You knew Frank? Why am I just hearing this now?" She looked as if he'd slapped her and maybe he had. "I don't recall him ever mentioning a Brody Jensen."

"We were on the same team together. They called me Hawk." Brody held his breath, waiting for the fallout from his admission.

"Hawk? You're Hawk." Confusion warred with hurt in her eyes. "Why didn't you just tell me?"

Brody sighed and squeezed her hands tighter, more for his own comfort than hers. "He asked me to check on you if anything ever happened to him, to make sure you were okay."

"Why didn't you just tell me?" she repeated.

He swallowed and told her the truth. The hardest words he'd ever said. "I was there when it—it happened. I'd been hit by a tracer round and was down. He came out of his cover and dragged me to safety but not before he took a few hits himself. They medivacked me out of there a few hours later, but he—he never made it. His wounds were fatal."

"You're the one he saved." She spoke in a deadly quiet voice. "You're the one he gave his life for."

Brody nodded, unable to speak. His chest constricted, making every breath painful.

"I need a few minutes alone." Mandy pulled her hands from his and walked out onto the porch into the cold night. Brody let her go, and he let his future leave with her.

He put his head in his hands and closed his eyes.

It was over.

* * * *

Mandy stared at the water lapping the shore of Fiddler's Cove. She leaned on the railing and closed her eyes, listening to the sounds of the night.

Part of her wanted to blame Brody, but she couldn't blame him. She just couldn't. He'd carried this secret with him for the past several months, blaming himself for Frank's death, taking it on himself because that was the kind of man he was. Yet, she couldn't blame him, couldn't hold him responsible for Frank's actions because he wasn't responsible.

She heard the door open and Brody's steps behind her. "Are you okay?"

Mandy turned and went to him, cupping his face in her

hands. "I don't blame you."

He stared into her eyes, leaned forward, and planted a feather soft kiss on her lips. "I believe you, but it doesn't change anything. I'm leaving in the morning."

"I want you to stay. Everyone loves you. The team adores you. You're part of this town now, of my family."

"Exactly why I can't stay. I'll break your heart even worse if I do. This is no place for me. You know my type. I can't do this to you again. Someday I may well come home in a body bag."

"I handled it once. I can handle it again."

"You weren't handling it very well when I showed up here." He shook his head, maintaining his resolve even when the devastation in her eyes must have made it damn near impossible.

She moved to him and wrapped her arms around him. "You said you loved me."

"Yeah, I do," he whispered against her lips, seeming close to caving, but he didn't. Unfortunately for her, he was made of stronger stuff than that. "I have to go. You'll find someone else more appropriate. This is the right thing for you and because I love you, I'm going to do the right thing."

"No," she cried out, her heart splintering into millions of irreparable pieces.

"I'm sorry." Brody gently pushed her away and shook his head. "I need to go."

"Now?" She almost looked panic-stricken.

"Yeah, now. It's best."

She started to argue, but he held up a hand and stopped her. "Let's each keep our dignity intact. I'll pack and be out of your hair in a half hour."

With a gut-wrenching sob, she grabbed her car keys and purse and ran out the door, unable to bear watching him pack and walk out of her life one last time.

Chapter 20—Homecoming

Brody lay in the cot and stared out the window at the stars dotting the Middle-Eastern sky, stars similar, yet foreign, to the ones he'd stared at countless times in the past few months on Madrona Island.

Madrona Island.

Brody pushed the thoughts of the beautiful island and the dark haired woman from his mind and attempted to recount the day's events—the morning spent translating some communications and the afternoon questioning some farmers on the locations of certain terrorist cells. He found translating to be deadly dull and boring. The questioning didn't do much for him either. With his bum leg, he'd never be sent out into the field, unless you called this godforsaken place, *the field*. Some would. Some wouldn't.

Unable to sleep, he pulled on his pants and coat and walked outside to pace the small courtyard in the walled compound. His feet raised puffs of sand. The cold desert night bit into his skin and his breath hung in the frigid air. Not a blade of grass anywhere. Certainly not a bay or any sign of water.

Before he'd gone to Madrona Island, he'd looked forward to this assignment, even though he'd be confined mostly to this compound. Somehow the reality of it didn't match his expectations. He got off on coaching a bunch of high school kids more than he got off on being in this place. A lot more.

He stopped, clasped his hands behind his back, and gazed up at those stars, wishing he was gazing up at the same stars only on the other side of the world.

He didn't want to be here, which shocked him. He'd never considered that he might have lost his passion for this job, that he might want to do something else with his life, or that his heart might actually be a thousand miles away instead of here craving danger and duty.

He'd done his duty and done it well. He'd paid the price,

made the sacrifices. Now he wanted to move on.

Brody wanted a life, a normal, everyday life, the same type of life he'd once considered boring and not for him. He imagined the alternative to this. He'd come home from work, walk in the house, and kiss his wife on the mouth. Hell, maybe he'd dip her down and make it one hell of a kiss. Maybe they'd never get to dinner and leave it to burn in the oven as they headed for the bedroom. He'd coach football, make lasting friendships, hang out with the guys on Sundays watching the game. He'd have a couple kids, a little boy and a little girl, one who looked just like Mandy with those soulful brown eyes. He'd spoil her rotten because he couldn't refuse her.

Brody waited for the claustrophobia to set in, warning him as it always did that such a life wasn't for a guy like him.

Nothing happened except for a soul-deep yearning for a future he'd walked away from, one far more exciting and challenging than this life he lived in the desert and barren hills of a foreign country.

He wanted to go home—to his home—his and Mandy's.

* * * *

Mandy forced a laugh at one of Parker's dramatic stories. Her youngest brother knew how to spin a good tale, not to mention being a natural-born charmer. Of course, every woman in town fell under his spell, young and old alike.

She glanced at her other two brothers. Case and Caleb stood near the fireplace mantle recounting the state championship with Connor. Caro stared at Case with rare want written all over her face. Aunt Kat bustled around the packed living room, filling appetizer trays and doling out more alcohol. Mandy's mother ran between the kitchen and the living room as the smells of prime rib wafted through the air. The noise levels in the room rose as various aunts, uncles, and cousins fought to be heard in their various side conversations.

The perfect Christmas Eve in her newly remodeled bed

and breakfast. Except—

Mandy squashed that thought but it bounced right back into her head like a hard rubber ball. Brody was gone. For good. She'd not heard a word from him since he'd walked out the door a few weeks ago.

Her mother and aunt kept glancing at her, as if expecting her to break down in tears at any moment. Even Case had patted her on the shoulder and said, "I miss him, too. He was a helluva football coach and could've been a good friend."

Mandy would give herself some time to get over it, move on, and make something of her life. She'd already enrolled in some correspondence courses to get her teaching degree. She patted herself on the back for not falling into her usual food-drugged depression. Instead of over-eating, she'd put her energy into going for walks and exercising. She'd actually lost another couple of pounds. She'd never be model thin, but she'd make a size ten or die trying.

Brody would be proud. The thought stuck in her chest like a sharp kitchen knife from the butcher block of expensive knives in her mother's kitchen.

Sniffling, she rubbed her eyes and hoped no one noticed. Standing, she walked to the Christmas tree, twinkling with lights and overloaded with ornaments. Keeping her back to the family, she pretended to be examining some of the older ornaments while she gathered her composure. Every ornament on this tree told a story. The macaroni strand of garland she'd made in first grade. The merit badge Case earned in Boy Scouts. A hula girl from Parker's senior trip to Hawaii. Antique glass ornaments from Grandma's tree. The angel her father bought for his first Christmas with his wife.

Mandy wanted to make memories like that for her husband and kids.

Someday.

She fingered the clear glass ball with the Santa inside it and couldn't remember a time it didn't adorn the family's tree.

Over the din in the room, Mandy heard the doorbell rang.

He mother hustled into the entryway to welcome the latest guest. A second later then entire room hushed. Mandy turned, shocked at the sudden silence and received a bigger shock. Her heart swelled in her chest. She blinked her eyes several times, certain she was seeing a mirage. Her knees wobbled and she gripped the back of a chair to steady herself.

It couldn't be. He was in the Middle East.

Yet there he was.

Brody stood across the quiet room, while Bing Crosby sang *I'll be Home for Christmas* over the stereo. He clasped his hands in front of him and stared at her warily, as if not sure what to expect.

Her feet had set anchor and refused to budge. Brody limped across the room to her as all eyes in the room followed him. A lone tear trickled down her cheek and must have given him the needed courage because he dropped to one knee in front of her. Not an easy feat for a man with knees like his.

He took her hand in his sweaty one and gazed up at her. Love shone in his eyes, just like it did in hers. "I'm back, Mandy. For good. I realized I could get all the excitement I need right here. With you. With all of you." He paused to look around the room. Case gave him a thumbs up and nodded at Mandy.

"Okay."

"I love you. I want us to make a life together. Will you marry me?"

"What?" She stared down at him and the small, open box containing a conservative diamond ring.

"Will you marry me?" His uncertain yet hopeful expression warmed her heart. He couldn't possibly think she'd say no.

"Yes. Yes. Yes." She shouted her answer, and threw her arms around him, toppling him to the floor and her with him. Brody wrapped his arms around her, and she knew the truth of it all. He'd come home for good.

All around her the applause of family and friends echoed

in her ears. Yes, it was time. A time to begin again. A new life. A new love. And a bright future watching Madrona sunsets from Fiddlers Cove.

~ THE END ~

Thank you for spending time in my world. I hope you enjoyed reading this book. If you did, please help other readers discover this book by leaving a review.

COMPLETE BOOKLIST

The following Jami Davenport titles are available in electronic and some are available in trade paperback format.

Madrona Island Series
Madrona Sunset

Evergreen Dynasty Series
Save the Last Dance
Who's Been Sleeping in My Bed?
The Gift Horse

Game On in Seattle—Seattle Sockeyes Hockey
Skating on Thin Ice
Crashing the Boards
Crashing the Net (Coming Soon)

Seattle Lumberjacks Football Series
Fourth and Goal
Forward Passes
Down by Contact
Backfield in Motion
Time of Possession
Roughing the Passer

Standalone Books
Christmas Break
Love at First Snow

ABOUT THE AUTHOR

If you'd like to be notified of new releases, special sales, and contests, subscribe here: **http://eepurl.com/LpfaL**

USA Today Bestselling Author Jami Davenport is an advocate of happy endings and writes sexy contemporary and sports romances, including her two new indie endeavors: the Game On in Seattle Series and the Madrona Island Series. Jami's new releases consistently rank in the top fifty on the sports romance and sports genre lists on Amazon, and she has hit the Amazon top hundred authors list in both contemporary romance and genre fiction multiple times.

Jami lives on a small farm near Puget Sound with her Green Beret-turned-plumber husband, a Newfoundland cross with a tennis ball fetish, a prince disguised as an orange tabby cat, and an opinionated Hanoverian mare.

Jami works in IT for her day job and is a former high school business teacher. She's a lifetime Seahawks and Mariners fan and is waiting for the day professional hockey comes to Seattle. An avid boater, Jami has spent countless hours in the San Juan Islands, a common setting in her books. In her opinion, it's the most beautiful place on earth.

Website: http://www.jamidavenport.com
Events Blog: http://jamidavenport.blogspot.com
Romancing the Jock Blog: http://www.romancingthejock.com
Twitter Address: @jamidavenport
Facebook: http://www.facebook.com/jamidavenport
Facebook Fan Page:
   http://www.facebook.com/jamidavenportauthor
Pinterest: http://pinterest.com/jamidavenport/

Goodreads: http://www.goodreads.com/author/show/1637218.Jami_Davenport

Made in the USA
Middletown, DE
26 January 2017